SARAH   *ething
Beginning With, *Tell Me Everything* and *Getting The Picture*,
and two collections of short stories, *Leading the Dance* and
the experimental collaboration, *Messages*. She lives in London
and is currently the RFL Fellow at the London School of
Economics and Political Science.

www.sarahsalway.com

Also by Sarah Salway

Something Beginning With
Getting the Picture
Leading the Dance
Messages

SARAH SALWAY

Tell Me Everything

FRIDAY BOOKS

The Friday Project
An imprint of HarperCollins*Publishers*
77–85 Fulham Palace Road
Hammersmith
London W6 8JB

www.thefridayproject.co.uk
www.harpercollins.co.uk

This edition published by The Friday Project 2010

A version of this book was first published by Bloomsbury in 2006

ISBN 978-0-00-737126-6

Set in Minion by Palimpsest Book Production Limited,
Falkirk, Stirlingshire

Printed and bound in Great Britain by Clays Ltd, St Ives plc

 Mixed Sources
Product group from well-managed
forests and other controlled sources
www.fsc.org Cert no. SW-COC-001806
FSC © 1996 Forest Stewardship Council

FSC is a non-profit international organisation established to promote the
responsible management of the world's forests. Products carrying the FSC
label are independently certified to assure consumers that they come
from forests that are managed to meet the social, economic and
ecological needs of present and future generations.

Find out more about HarperCollins and the environment at
www.harpercollins.co.uk/green

Find yourself a cup of tea; the
teapot is behind you. Now tell
me about hundreds of things.

Saki

You can tell me anything, she said.

And I believed her.

I only have your best interests at heart, my biology teacher told me. It'll go no further unless I consider you at risk.

There are moments when you really can stop time. Make a decision to go one way, and not the other. There's just a sense, a prickle on the skin, something impossible to describe, that tells you you're at the crossroads. But it's only when you're too far along to change direction that you realise you ever had a choice.

So, lulled by the warmth in the biology lab and the novelty of an adult really listening to me, I spent the afternoon telling her stories. In the cosy web I wove there, I lost sense of where I began and she ended. We seemed to be in it together; my words pulling expressions out of her face that made me want to carry on, to take the two of us higher and higher up a ladder of emotions. I was filled with something outside myself. I didn't have to think, to struggle and stumble in the middle of a sentence for a thought or a word, not even once. I was floating. It was only when we reached the top that I realised how exhausting it can be to empty yourself out.

When it was time to go home I stood in the doorway, not wanting to cross the threshold back into the outside world.

'I can come here again, can't I?' I asked. 'We can do this another time, can't we?'

I was watching the tears falling down her cheeks. They looked like icicles dropping off her chin. It made me want to laugh, but I was proud too. Proud that I'd made her feel that much. On the wall behind her there was a poster of a dissected human heart. All the tubes coming from it were left dangling in mid air. Cut off with a bloodless straight line.

By the time I got home, she'd already spoken to the headmistress who had rung my mother, and nothing was ever quite the same again. Not even the blood that pumped through our bodies, not even the air we all breathed. Everything had become thick, hard to absorb. It iced up the inside of our throats until we longed for any kind of warmth, even the fiercest hottest words that burn you in hell. At least they would melt the silence.

That's how I learnt the power of stories.

ONE

'How did you meet?'

People always ask you this when you become part of a couple. It's throat-clearing, before they get to the really interesting stuff which normally involves what *they* think about things, or how *they* met their partners, or just anything about *them* really.

Miranda was different though. She was only about a year older than I was, but was already a hairdresser in the salon near to the stationery shop where I worked. We met in the street where we were both forced to smoke our cigarettes. We were furtive, trying to look as if we didn't mind being outside. 'We're fag hags,' I said to her when we got to know each other better, but she never found this as funny as I did.

'You'd look lovely with your hair thinned,' she said to me the first day, after we'd been shuffling round and nodding at each other from our respective doorways for a bit.

I stubbed my cigarette out quickly and went back inside. I hoped I had smiled at her too but I've been told that sometimes when I try too hard, or am taken by surprise, my attempts at a friendly expression come out as grimaces. Ones I can't get rid of for a long time afterwards. My mouth gets so dry, it's as if my face has frozen with all my teeth bared.

Her words stayed in my head though, and a bit later I nipped into the toilet to look in the mirror. I brushed the hair away from my face and practised being normal. I pinched the ends

3

of my hair with my fingers to try to understand what she meant.

I tried to see myself as Miranda must have seen me.

Bright.

Interesting.

Someone else. Someone different.

And, let's face it, that's always an attraction.

After lunch, I made myself go out for my usual afternoon cigarette and hang around until Miranda appeared although I could see Mr Roberts gesturing from inside the shop. Although it was Mr Roberts's shop and I'd only been working there for a week by that time, I already knew he didn't like face-to-face customers. They might ask him something he didn't know the answer to but, as he said, it was water off a duck's back for me. Apparently he'd never known anyone who knew less than I did.

We were like those weather-house couples, Miranda and I, that afternoon. As soon as she popped out of her door, I went back into mine to put Mr Roberts out of his misery, but not before I managed to say, as casually as I could:

'Do you really think so then?'

'What?'

'I should thin my hair?'

'Definitely. Come in to the salon on Wednesday. It's model night.'

After that first time, the Wednesday model night, turned out so disastrously, Miranda promised to work on my image a bit more gradually.

I had been worried she might give up on me when I lost my nerve in the middle of all those other women and ran out of the salon halfway through with the soapsuds still in my hair, so when she came up to me in the street the following morning and asked me for a light, I was going to explain about how it got too much hearing all those women's voices, the words floating around me, clinging to me. I was even going to tell her about the biology teacher and what had happened but before I could say anything, she cut me off. She suggested that maybe the next time we should do it more privately. To take it easy. To change more slowly. As if it really could be that simple. As if there was nothing more to say.

So after that, I started going across the road to Miranda's most nights after I finished work, and she'd put on a selection of sad echoey ballads. They filled up the empty salon and would make us feel all full up and weepy too. We'd smoke our cigarettes in that warm muggy atmosphere, spinning round on the seats and flicking our ash into the basins as the street darkened outside. There was a female smell in the air: the chemical tartness of hairspray, a garden of roses and lilies from the shampoos and underneath it, a dampness from the dying bouquets left just a day too long on the reception desk. While she leafed through magazines and read out horrific stories to me, I'd look in the mirror and try to see myself as Miranda did.

'See her.' She pointed out a photograph of an ordinary looking middle-aged woman smiling for the camera. 'Attacked in broad daylight by a man with a sharpened broom handle who split her stomach from throat to bum, she was. Can't do housework now. Says sweeping brings back nasty memories. There's pictures of the scar too. Want to look?'

And in between murders and misery, she'd show me photographs of beautiful women she would say I was the spitting image of if only I would agree to let her transform me.

'You're stunning,' she said. 'I'd kill for your eyes.'

That was how we talked to each other, Miranda and I. As if we were practising for one of those Sunday afternoon black and white films mum always used to watch. 'I'd die with joy if I could have your nose,' I lied. 'It's like Doris Day. It's sweet. If your nose was a person it would wear a frilly apron.'

'Oh but your ears. They'd wear black berets with diamond studs on them. There's something decidedly glamorous about your ears.'

'Do you think so?'

'And your cheeks. They're the Kylie Minogue of cheeks. So, so, so...cheeky.'

I peered in the mirror, trying to read something more into the outline of my face than just that. An outline. What *was* it that Miranda could see?

'We should go out one time,' she said, 'to the cinema or something.'

'Or to the pub?' I suggested.

'I don't think so,' she laughed. 'Nasty loud places. No, we'll find a nice romantic comedy. Something jolly, that's the ticket.'

Neither of us had boyfriends when we first met.

We would talk about men though, but always in that 'oh aren't they hopeless' way other women did. I'd talk about Mr Roberts, but I didn't tell Miranda everything. To make her laugh I'd ham it up about how he got me to go up the stepladder to fetch down boxes from the top shelf. Miranda and I grimaced at each other when I demonstrated the way he'd hold on to my legs when I was up there, and how he said he did it because he was scared I might topple over but we both knew he was fibbing.

'I'm not surprised though,' Miranda said. 'Your calf muscles are perfect. You should insure your legs. I've never seen such romantic legs.'

'Oh you,' I cooed. This was something I'd learnt to do from Miranda. Cooing, and saying: 'Oh you.'

When I got back to my room though, I couldn't resist lifting up my skirts and having a quick look at my legs in the mirror. I turned this way and that, trying to see the romance Miranda must have read there. I flexed my legs, letting my fingers trail over where muscles should be. I shut my eyes so I wouldn't have to see the dimples of fat. I couldn't stop thinking about how Mr Roberts always said he liked a girl you could get hold of.

I sat on my bed later and watched the few passers-by in the street below as I ate my supper. I sipped my packet soup from my mug, pretending it was home-made and that I couldn't taste the chemicals of the mix. The doughnuts I picked delicately one by one from their box, licking my lips to catch the sugar from round my mouth. The last one I had to force down but I didn't want there to be any gaps in my body left unfilled.

It was so quiet. Blissfully, eerily quiet, in my little upstairs room. When it was time to sleep, I lay down and placed my hands in the form of a cross on my chest. The only sound was the occasional echo of footsteps which drifted up from the street. Some running, others dawdling. Everyone going home, I thought.

TWO

'How did you meet?' This was the first thing Miranda asked when I told her about Tim.

We were in the salon. Miranda was putting my hair up into a high pleat. I could feel her fingernails scrape against my scalp as she twisted strands into shape.

I couldn't get the words out. All I'd told her so far was that I had a boyfriend called Tim, but now I kept giggling. I hid behind my hand as I tried to answer Miranda.

I'd had a hard time even just saying 'boyfriend'. It didn't feel right. Not next to Tim. Somehow Tim and Boyfriend weren't two words that went naturally together. So by the time I'd finally managed to say it all in just the one sentence she was suspicious. That's why her question wasn't just throat-clearing. She really wanted to know.

I spun the back of the empty hairdressing chair next to me so I wouldn't have to look at Miranda's face in the mirror. In the background Miss Otis was busy regretting how she wasn't going to be able, after all, to make lunch.

'In the park,' I said. Round and round the chair spun.

'What are you reading?' Tim had asked, and I showed him the second-hand romance I'd just picked up from the charity shop. I didn't let him judge my reading habits from the pale pink cover though. I told him how I was getting through Proust but the books were too heavy to carry around. The novels I read outside

9

were lighter. Not just in weight. They helped me keep my concentration keen for the main task. I was determined to get through the whole of French literature by the time I was thirty, I said. That gave me years, I added. I wanted to get that in quickly. Because of my size, and because I'm still wearing the clothes my father bought me, most people think I'm a lot older than I am. This has worked in my favour recently, but there was something nice about wanting to be young again. I felt a lightness inside.

'The main task,' Tim repeated. 'You're keeping your concentration keen for the main task.' He nodded a lot as he said it so I could tell he liked that particular phrase. Maybe even that he liked me.

Tim didn't say much, but he never stopped moving. He tapped his fingers on his jeans as if he was playing the piano, his feet twitched up and down too in a rhythm I tried to catch. He was wearing no socks. It was one of the first things I noticed about him.

A man passed us as we sat there. 'Nice day,' he said, or something like that, and I smiled back. Tim's feet stayed still then, I noticed. His ankles were white and bony above his unlaced trainers. A vein snaked its way round the bump like a twisting river of blood.

'You're not saying you picked someone up in the park!'

I came back to Miranda's salon with a start.

'Do you not know how dangerous that is? Do you not know that, Molly? There was this woman in one of my magazines who was captured by a man she met in the park. He kept her like a dog in a flat nearby, let her out for exercise and she was so frightened that she always came back to him when he called. Can you not imagine that?' When Miranda got excited a Scottish undercurrent always came out, not just in the accent but in the sentence order too. The negativity of her Caledonian grammar made me more defensive than I knew I should have been.

'I can look after myself,' I said.

Miranda pulled a piece of my hair especially tight, ignoring my gasp. 'Leave that chair alone,' she said too, and I let go of it, but not before spinning it once more round for luck.

'I was just sitting on the Seize the Day bench reading,' I said. 'He came to sit there too. Asked if I had any idea who Jessica was.'

'Not local then.'

I shook my head. That had been one of the first things I'd thought too. All the locals knew about Jessica Carter. She was a teenage girl who had killed herself four years ago. It was just before she took her A levels and when she died, it started a big campaign about adolescent pressure at school and academic achievements and how girls were supposed to look like models as well as everything else.

Because that's what she wrote in her suicide note: *Maybe if I was prettier, then none of this would have mattered.*

No one but me seemed to think it was funny how the newspapers used the story as an excuse to print photographs of Jessica looking pretty alongside the articles about how dangerous it was to worry so much about appearance. My mother had told me not to always be so difficult, but it was true. There were lots of photographs, not just of Jessica but of film stars, supermodels, musicians. Pages and pages of beautiful women.

'Don't go all dreamy on me, Molly,' Miranda said. 'You were telling me about the man.'

'He's different,' I said. 'Hard to explain.'

'Could I meet him?'

'I'll ask but he's not shy exactly. More private.'

She shrugged and twisted my chair so I was sitting straight, facing the mirror with her standing behind me. I normally liked seeing us like that, one on top of the other like two twists in one of those fancy bread sticks they sell in the Italian deli on the corner but there was something strange about our reflections tonight.

'I thought we might go for a flick-out at the end of your hair next time,' she said. 'It'll bring out the beautiful texture of your skin. You've been blessed with your skin. It makes me mad with jealousy.'

I put my hand up to my neck in the mirror, let my finger and thumb stretch across so I could be strangling myself, but then raised my hand up so it was just cupping my chin. Softly. 'But your neck . . .' I said. Behind me, Miranda lifted her face up in the mirror to expose the arch of her neck.

THREE

I was pleased Tim was late for our date that night.

It gave me more time with Jessica.

'Jessica,' I told her in my head, tracing the carved letters on the rough wood of the bench with my fingertips as if I was playing the piano. S.E.I.Z.E. T.H.E. D.A.Y. There'd been a collection for the bench at school, but it was the headmaster who had chosen the words. He'd wanted it to be a lesson to spur the rest of us into a new joy of life, but it hadn't worked. Rather than the inspiration he'd hoped for, the Seize the Day bench had become a symbol for everything that could go wrong. I wondered whether that was why most people shied away from it. Most people, that is, apart from Tim and me. 'This is how I met him . . .'

And, although it all happened on her bench and she must have been aware of us, I told her everything Tim had said that first time I met him, and how when Tim asked whether we could meet again, I told him this bench could be our regular spot. 'Maybe tomorrow. I'm often here. She was a friend,' I'd lied to him.

After the first ripples of shock at Jessica's death had gone round the school, there was a curious quietness everywhere for weeks. Every excuse for not being happy was suddenly flawed.

'Maybe if I was prettier . . .' But if you were looking for one word to describe Jessica, it would have been pretty.

'Maybe if I had more money . . .' But Jessica's family took two holidays a year. Once, for her fourteenth birthday, they took the whole class to a theme park for her party. Jessica got all her clothes in London, not the local Topshop like the rest of us. She wasn't the sort of girl who needed a Saturday job.

'Maybe if I was cleverer . . .' But Jessica was a top A student.

But now, when no one else but me seemed to bother to visit the bench any more, things seemed more equal. 'We could have been friends,' I told Jessica. 'I used to be so unhappy as well.' D.A.Y. My index finger traced the scars in the wood made by the letters.

So perhaps that was why, even before Tim arrived, I was feeling as if I might have a bit of potential too. I put my face down and brushed my hair back over my shoulder with the side of my hand like Jessica used to do. After Jessica died, I used to do it at home so often that my father banned hair-touching at table. I couldn't have risked it at school either. It was definitely an in-crowd gesture, and might have drawn attention to me in a way my father wouldn't have liked.

I must have been too busy doing the hair thing to hear Tim come. When I looked up, he was already sitting down on the other end of the bench, his head between his knees.

'Are you OK?' I asked.

'Quick,' he said. 'Put your head down too. NOW!'

I copied him.

'Don't look up,' he warned. 'Shut your eyes if possible.'

I couldn't. I looked at the ground instead. There were bits of chewing gum stuck under the bench. Cigarette butts, even a beer bottle. I made up my mind to tidy up sometime. For Jessica's sake.

'Wha . . .'

'Be quiet,' Tim said. He put his arm round my shoulders to draw me closer to him. I could feel the heat of his body through his jumper. The outline of his fingers across my back burnt into me like infrared. He smelt of fabric conditioner and warm apples. I'd never been so close to a boy before. I tried hard to stop my body from tensing up, to relax more and enjoy the embrace.

'We're going to have to make a run for it,' Tim said. He stood up and held out his hand, and I took it, clutching at his fingers as he pulled me into the bushes that lined the edge of the park. Just when I was thinking I couldn't run any more, he stopped and we hid behind a tree for him to keep a watch out. He pulled the sleeves of his jumper down to cover my hands, holding on to my wrists so tightly. I did the same to him. It was as if we were grafting ourselves on to each other.

'I know who it is,' I said. 'It's my father. He's found me.'

Tim hushed me. 'It's not,' he replied. 'I'll keep you safe.'

I didn't ask how he could be so certain. My heart was beating hard against his chest and the echo travelled up to my head. I wondered if Tim could hear the same noises as I could. The scuffle of leaves as a squirrel hunted for nuts, a dog barking in a garden somewhere near, the distant sound of a train announcement from the station. No one walking past us would be able to see us in our nest of leaves. I wasn't sure how long we could stay there, not moving, but every time I tried to ask Tim what was happening, he put his lips down, hushing through my hair, his breath hot against my scalp.

We were so close, I smelt a flowery sweetness on his breath I couldn't identify. It was the first time anyone had held me like that since my mother stopped touching me. Since the biology teacher business. I tried not to cry, but just rested my weight against his chest, my head lying on the soft pad of his shoulder.

We didn't say anything. There didn't seem the need.

Eventually, he let go of my wrists and we walked out on to the path together. Across the far side there were a few houses with their top lights still on, but apart from that there was no sign of life.

'Will you?' I asked.

'What?'

'Keep me safe?'

Tim nodded. 'Tomorrow?' he asked.

I smiled. He put one hand on my head, stroked my hair gently and then without saying another word, he turned. I watched him leave the park. He walked quicker than other people. He knew where he was going. When I couldn't see him any more I sat back on the Seize the Day bench.

I wanted my heart to settle down before going back to Mr Roberts's shop.

FOUR

This is how I met Mr Roberts.

He caught me crying at one of the café tables they put up outside the Church on the High Street during spring and summer.

Despite the cold, I'd been sitting there for one hour, forty-two minutes refusing all offers of refreshments, even though I could see the volunteers pointing me out and tut-tutting amongst each other. Then a plump peachy woman came out wearing a white blouse and flowery skirt with one of those elasticated waists women her age wear for comfort although they're always having to hoist the skirt back down from where it's risen up under their tits. She told me I wasn't to sit there any more. That the café tables were for proper customers only.

I started to cry, and suddenly this old man came up and told the waitress it was all right. That I was with him.

It was Mr Roberts, although of course I didn't know that then. I was just relieved that everybody was now staring at him instead of me. He said nothing at first. Just bought me a cup of tea, pushed it over and sat there in silence until I raised my head.

'What do they mean about being proper?' I asked.

'I suppose they want people who'll pay,' he said. 'Although the Bible does have something to say about merchants in the temple.'

'I might not want anything to drink,' I said, 'but that doesn't mean I'm not proper. They should be more careful about what words they use. Words matter.'

'I know that, pet,' he replied. 'You don't want to worry about Church people. They've no taste. They can't see how special you are.'

This made me cry even harder. Mr Roberts didn't say anything, just got up so I thought he was leaving me too but he came back with a handful of paper napkins and handed them to me.

'Dry yourself,' he said. 'And then we'll sort you out.'

I wiped the tears away and looked up at him nervously, but he shook his head. 'Not yet,' he said, and pulled out a sheet of newspaper he had neatly folded away in the pocket of his tweed jacket. It was the racing pages and he started studying form closely.

He was right too. As soon as I realised his attention had wandered away from me, I started crying again, loud, gasping sobs. When he didn't seem to mind, I ignored the sour looks I was getting from the Church woman and let it all come out. The pile of napkins was sodden by the time I was finished and his racing columns were full of little biroed marks and comments. He must have been about sixty, with steely grey hair cut forward over a bulging forehead. It was his mouth I noticed most. It was prim and womanly with perfectly shaped teeth he kept tapping his pen against. It wasn't the first time I'd noticed that the older men get, the more feminine their mouths and chins become. It's the opposite of women, who start to sprout bristles and Winston Churchill jowls. In fact, most long-term married couples look as if they've swapped faces from the nose down. Morphing into each other's mother or father.

I coughed and he looked up. Then he looked again but slower, up and down my body. He even tilted his head to one side so he could get a gawp at my legs.

'Well, you're a big girl,' he said. 'What sort of weight would you say you were then?'

It wasn't funny, but I was so shocked by him coming out

with a statement like that, I just exploded into giggles. Since I'd put on all this weight, everybody pussy-footed around the subject. Fat-ism. But although I laughed I couldn't help it when, just as quickly, the tears started to well up again. Mr Roberts creased his eyes in annoyance so I tried to stop both the laughing and the crying.

'It's glandular,' I explained. 'I eat nothing really, but I can't help putting weight on. Mum says it runs in the family, although my father used to—' I stopped.

'Used to what?' He stared at me as if he was weighing me himself. 'So there's a mother and a father in the background. Been mean to you, have they, or is it boyfriend trouble?'

I shook my head. Since that afternoon in the biology room, I'd found that the hurricane of feelings continually raging inside me was impossible to put into words for anyone, let alone a stranger. That's why I'd come here, to get away from it all. I thought of the counsellor they made me see at my new school. The red chair I used to sit on for my weekly sessions with her, the box of ever-ready tissues like the ones I was clutching now.

'There are times when nothing goes right,' I told Mr Roberts, catching myself before I copied the counsellor's long vowels too strongly. 'This is just one of these times. I just need to sit it out, wait patiently and my turn to shine will come. Life is a wheel and sometimes we're on an upwards circle and sometimes we're heading down. It's all natural. Part of living. You can't fight it.'

He stared at me. 'Got a job?' he asked.

I shook my head. I was longing to pinch myself. It was one of my ways of coping when a conversation got out of hand. Normally this was fine because most of the conversations I'd had recently were just in my head but I knew pinching wasn't OK in public. Particularly not in a church. I contented myself with squeezing my fingernails hard against my palm instead. I tried not to wince with the pain.

'You're not at school, are you?'

I looked down at the table. I was longing to look at my palms and see the marks from my nails but couldn't risk it so I let my hands rest on my knees. 'Not any more,' I mumbled.

'Too much time. That's your trouble.'

I shrugged.

'Drugs? Alcohol?'

'No.'

'Sex?'

I stared at the sugar bowl so he couldn't how my red and hot my cheeks were. Sex wasn't something you talked about in public, let alone so near a church.

'Ah,' he said, as if he'd discovered something from my silence. 'So that's it. And no one understands you, that's the problem, is it?'

Silence.

'Living at home?'

I twisted a strand of my hair so tightly round my finger the skin went white. It looked as if I was trying to slice the top off, to get down to the bone.

'Stop doing that,' he told me. 'Where do you live then?'

'Nowhere,' I said. I held the wet tissues to my cheeks, the palm of my hand stuffed in my mouth so I wouldn't cry.

Mr Roberts prodded my duffle bag with the tip of his foot. 'Your mum chucked you out?' he asked.

I looked at him and then nodded. My stomach had been hardening into a knot as I answered his questions. The strange thing was that Mr Roberts was drawing a picture of me that I rather liked. I felt I was in one of those documentaries on the television. The waif the television crew found on a street corner and whose story they shared to make the viewers feel half-guilty, half-grateful for what life had thrown at her, and not them.

I smiled bravely. I expected Mr Roberts to be kind to me now.

'Can't say I'm surprised if the only sentences you can manage to string together are about wheels and that crap,' he said. 'Or is she as bad as you? Is that where you caught it from? Psychobabble. Nothing worse.'

I opened my mouth to reply, but he put his hand up to hush me. 'I can just imagine the set-up. Wind chimes, patchouli and no discipline. Yoga even.' He spat the word out as if it were a bad taste he wanted rid of. 'So where are you staying tonight?'

I started to get up. 'Thank you for the tea,' I said. Just because he was so rude, it didn't mean I couldn't remember my manners.

'No, you don't.' He put his hand on my shoulder and pushed me back down. I looked round for the Church woman but now that I needed her she was busy sorting out the plastic teaspoons by size. It seemed to be taking every last bit of her concentration, although I noticed she was keeping in earshot. 'You're not quite what I thought but there's something about you. Do you know how to keep quiet?'

I nodded.

'Thought so. Had to learn, have you?'

I nodded again.

'And how old are you?' he asked.

'Twenty-five,' I lied.

He raised his eyebrows at me questioningly but I held my chin up.

'I've a room above the shop you can kip down in temporarily if you want,' he said. 'Do you?'

I fiddled with the packet of sugar until he repeated himself, but louder.

'Well, do you want it?'

Another nod. In my mind I was still the street-waif and this was just one more step along my journey, either down to degradation or back up with the clean shiny people. Only time would tell. I was a dandelion wisp twirled around in the wind of fate.

'Although there are conditions,' he continued.

I thought about how the girl in the television documentary would be used to conditions. I nodded again.

FIVE

The room Mr Roberts offered me was bare and uncarpeted. There was already a mattress up there, and Mr Roberts came in the next day with a sleeping bag he said I could have. Although it still had the price tag on, he told me it was an old one he didn't want any more. There was some relief in his pretence that he was doing nothing for me really. It meant I could slip into my new life quietly, without too much obligation to anyone.

I made myself a dressing table out of a few of the boxes of old stationery stored in the room, and piled the others against one wall so they acted as a makeshift shelf. I covered them with a piece of old blue curtain material I'd found in a skip in one of the roads being gentrified behind the High Street.

The same skip yielded a broken coat stand that I painted with paint returned from a stationery order that had apparently gone wrong. It wasn't surprising an office didn't want it, because it was bright pink. 'Nice for a girl though,' Mr Roberts said when he handed it over. Again, I wondered if he'd bought it especially for me.

A couple of rubber bands and a ball of string stopped the coat stand falling apart, and I used it instead of a wardrobe to hang up the few clothes I had. When I saw how successful this was, I painted the woodwork around the window pink, and then the door, the pretty fireplace that was left over from better times, and I even drew crooked pink stripes down one wall. The room felt a bit like a drunken beach-hut, but I liked it.

One of the first things Miranda did was to give me a cracked full-length mirror from the salon which I hung on the wall, hiding it behind a curtain of the same blue material as my dressing table so I didn't have to look at myself the whole time. She also offered me some old hair and celebrity magazines, and I spent several evenings cutting out photographs of women I admired from them. I was careful to follow the lines of their hairstyles exactly as I knew this would matter to Miranda but the bodies I often sliced through, making them all even slimmer and more stick-like than they really were. These I plastered up on the wall, one on top of the other so when I lay in the mattress on the floor that acted as my bed, it felt as if they were all tumbling down on me.

In the middle of these perfect women, I slotted the one photograph of my mother that I'd brought with me. She stood out only slightly, and more because of the shininess of the photographic paper than a lack of beauty on her part. I felt proud of her up there with the beautiful people. There was something about the way she seemed to belong there that made me hope she got a second chance to do what she wanted now I wasn't messing up her life any more. I hugged myself tightly whenever I had this thought because it always made me cry. I'd lie on my back and let my fingers rest on the outline of her hair sometimes, stroking it in the way I would have liked Miranda to do with mine but could never come out and ask for straight. In the photo, Mum had her arms out slightly as if she was calling for someone. It could have been anyone haring towards her, but I knew it was me she was beckoning.

I tacked the rest of the material up above the mattress so it hung down like a canopy keeping the world out.

No one came into the room but me, but I spent a lot of time there. I ate and slept and read and thought there. Washing took place in the hand-basin in the little loo downstairs that we used for the shop, so four times already I'd walked up to the local leisure centre and had a proper shower. By the time I met Tim, I hadn't had a bath for nearly two weeks but I kept telling myself firmly that what you don't have, you don't miss. When I was younger, I used to spend so long in the bath my father always said my skin would crinkle up and fall off.

'And then where would you be?' he yelled once from the other side of the bathroom door.

'Here,' I shouted back. I was furious. Would he never leave me alone? 'I'll still be here.'

'No one would want you,' he said then. 'Not without your covering. You'd be a mess of bloody insides. That's all. Nothing to hold you all together. You certainly wouldn't be my Molly.'

'And what if that's exactly what I don't want to be?' I'd asked then, from behind the safety of a locked door.

But he couldn't have heard me. There was no reply.

SIX

There were three boxes on the top shelf in the backroom of the stationery shop. On the second day I was there, Mr Roberts put up the 'Closed' sign and asked me to look for things that weren't in these boxes while he held the ladder tight. And if, while I was up there, I wanted to tell him all the naughty things I'd been up to – *a great big girl like you* – then Mr Roberts wouldn't mind.

No sir-ree, he wouldn't mind at all.

So these were the conditions he'd mentioned. It took me some time to get the hang of this exchange of 'information'. The first time, after he made it as clear as Mr Roberts ever would what he wanted me to do, I had to think hard of what I could tell him. It would be safer to stick to stuff about the girls at school, I decided, and the funny thing was I knew straight away what my first one should be. This was a story that shocked me so much it had felt like a physical blow when I first heard it. Telling Mr Roberts seemed like a good way to get it finally out of my mind.

So, standing on top of the ladder, I was almost eager as I recited word for word the story of how pretty, clever, popular Sylvia Collins got drunk on cider at a year eleven disco and four boys from the rugby team took her into the changing rooms and made her give them blow jobs, one by one, while the others looked on. And how after they'd finished with her, they took all her clothes and left her there, crying on the floor of the shower, while they went back to the disco to dance with the nice girls who were waiting for them.

'Did they dance with you?' Mr Roberts asked me.

'I didn't go to the disco. My dad never let me go to dances,' I said, but I'd realised something else I hadn't thought about before. That, even with all her potential, Sylvia was never seen back at school after the disco. I wondered if it was the nice girls who had made sure of that.

Mr Roberts let go of the ladder. 'That's enough for today, Molly,' he said. 'When we do this again maybe you could try to think of something of your own. And perhaps you could be, ah, a little more delicate.' And he went to fiddle with the cash register in the shop while I clambered down gracelessly.

I thought I'd got it sussed the second time.

This was more my own story, even if I had been just a spectator. But that had been the whole point of it, I told Mr Roberts.

All the boys in school had fancied Christine Chambers. She had curly black hair and a snub nose. Her eyes were green, and although she wasn't bright, she appeared to listen in class so she wasn't told off as much as the others in her group. Strangely this only added to her allure, because she used her popularity with the teachers to lessen punishments for her friends.

Christine's only obvious form of rebellion was a thin leather cord of brightly coloured beads she wore around her neck although no jewellery was allowed with the school uniform. With this necklace, she'd draw attention to herself in lessons, running her hands over the beads, pulling them this way and that, up to her lips. One day though, in history, she pulled so hard it broke and the beads spilled everywhere, noisily, over the wooden floor of the classroom, dancing this way, that way. Anxious for any diversion, we'd all thrown ourselves whooping on to the ground hunting for the runaway plastic jewels.

* * *

'Even you?' Mr Roberts asked. 'Can someone of your size throw themselves anywhere? I'd have liked to have seen that.' He cupped my calves with his open palms. 'Potatoes,' he groaned. 'Big fat potatoes. All mashed up tight in your naughty nylons.'

I shifted on the ladder so he couldn't hold on to me quite so tightly.

'Well, I haven't always been this exact shape but no, I wasn't on the floor,' I admitted. 'That's how I could watch what was going on.'

The only person – only other person, I corrected myself – who didn't leave her chair was Christine. So I'd been on the right level to see how, with her classmates scrambling round her feet, she fixed her eyes on the history teacher and lingeringly, slowly, she licked her lips and laughed silently at him. He smiled back and he almost seemed not to be aware of how his fingers went up to his neck and traced a line where a necklace might be. He looked as if he might be cutting his throat. Then, still without breaking the spell between them, he put his index finger to his lips and half blew her a kiss, which he transformed into a sigh as he noticed me sitting there.

'And that's it then? That's all that happened?' Mr Roberts said after I'd been silent for a moment.

'It was sex, the way they did it,' I explained. 'There must have been something going on between them.'

'Maybe you were imagining it. I know all about a young lady's imagination.'

'Maybe. But I know what I saw.'

'But it still wasn't you, Molly. That is the whole point of these stories. I thought I explained all that.'

I felt my throat ice over, and Mr Roberts jumped to one side as I almost fell down the ladder then. I think I took him by surprise.

Apart from the leg-holding and the occasional brush-past in the shop, he never touched me. I was grateful for that, but my attempts at storytelling were obviously disappointing to him. If I didn't get on track soon, I was frightened he might start demanding satisfaction for my board and lodgings in other ways.

That night, up in my room, I emptied my purse out on to the floor and stacked up the few coins into piles I could count. I carefully smoothed out the one note and placed it to the side.

Mr Roberts wasn't paying me a regular wage. Instead, he would keep the till open after a customer had been in and silently hand me a ten pound note when he felt like it. I'd slip it into my pocket without even a thank you and that would be that. He said that doing it any other way would only attract unnecessary attention and that I could trust him to see me all right.

By my bed I kept the book Mum had been reading the day I'd left home. I don't know what made me steal it from her bedside table but on my third day at the stationery shop, I took a sharp craft knife from one of the displays and cut a hole carefully through the inside pages. I opened the cover now and checked the cash that I'd hidden was still safe. I raised the book to my face and flicked the pages so they brushed my cheek. Their cut edges felt like the flutter of wings, almost a kiss, against my skin.

And then after I put the coins back into my purse, I took the torch Mr Roberts had given me and went down to wash myself at the sink in the toilet. I hated turning on the bright strip lighting after the shop was shut, taking comfort in the almost secret existence I was leading. After I finished rinsing my hands in the sink exactly six times, I folded my flannel precisely, each corner matching. At least there were still some things I was in charge of.

It was only much later, when I couldn't sleep, I gave in to the ache of needing to pinch myself, over and over, right at the top of my thighs, on the soft plump skin that no one would ever see. I wanted the comfort of the pain, so unbearable I didn't have to think of anything else. At least until the next pinch.

SEVEN

I was sitting in the empty salon with Miranda one evening soon after, watching her straighten her hair as we listened to Bryan Ferry murdering the old ballads.

'I'm after that shake your head look,' she said as she twisted over uncomfortably to one side. I could see the muscle on her neck work its way through her flesh in protest. 'When your hair looks as if it's a piece of cardboard that goes from side to side, and people get out of the way in case you slice them in half.'

I nodded as if I understood. There was a useful trick I first learnt during those school counselling sessions. When people start talking about something they're interested in but you're not, you have to empty yourself of any attempt to enter into the dialogue and just let the language float around you. If you're lucky some words stick, and what you do then is repeat them straight back. It doesn't seem to matter what order they come out in. When the counsellor used to get on one of her explaining jags and I did this, she'd clap her hands and say we were finally getting somewhere.

'So you're just trying to look as if you can slice some cardboard,' I said to Miranda, and she nodded as vigorously as she could with her hair trapped in the straighteners.

'I'll do it for you if you want,' she said.

'I've got a friend with this problem,' I said, quickly changing the subject. 'Someone wants her to tell him dirty stories, but she doesn't know any. It's not really her thing.'

33

'And this someone is your friend's boyfriend?' she asked, her left eyebrow arching in the mirror as she steadied her head the better to look at me.

'God no!' I said but then corrected myself. 'No, but it's important my friend gets it right. It's like a work thing, that's all. It's not kinky or anything.'

Miranda went back to stretching her hair, but I could tell she was thinking by the way her body had gone all alert. I squeezed little dollops of shampoo from the shelf onto my hand and inhaled them as I waited for her to speak.

Apple. Rosemary and pine. Honey. I stopped trying to make my skin absorb the liquid, just kept adding more and more on to the surface until my fingertips were swimming in oily goo. Then I went to get a clean towel from one of the piles in the back room to wipe it all off.

'We had this English teacher at school,' Miranda said when I came back. 'What he always said when we were writing stories was that it didn't matter if the facts were true or not, but whether we believed in them. For lots of reasons, it's something I've remembered.'

She paused then and I thought about what she'd just said. 'So you can make something true just by believing it?' I asked. 'What if you believe in a lie? It doesn't make sense.'

'I know,' Miranda sighed. 'But the way he explained it was that not everything's black and white. He used to ask us if we'd ever been nervous about waiting for something and how five minutes could seem like hours.'

I nodded.

'Well, what he said was that if you were trying to tell someone about it, you were better to say you had to wait five hours because that gave a more truer picture of what it felt like, even though it wasn't true.'

'And that's not bad?' The skin all over my body felt as if it was being charged by several hundred electric shocks. I willed Miranda to continue and after a few seconds – seconds that felt like hours – she did.

Miranda shook her head. 'In real life, it can be very bad,' she said. 'It can even ruin lives. But these are just stories we're talking about, aren't they?'

I stared at her. I couldn't speak.

Miranda clicked her tongue against the top of her mouth hard. 'Molly,' she said. I guessed she meant to be kind, even encourage me to say something more, but it took me out of the trance I was in danger of falling into. My cheeks were red from the heat in the salon and I could feel a flush coming up my neck. It was exactly as it had been in the school room.

'It was only something a friend told me,' I interrupted her before she could say anything else. 'What you're talking about reminded me of her.' I was willing myself not to cry. Next to me Miranda was holding the hairbrush at chin level, her mouth open. She looked as if she was about to sing into a microphone but no sound came out.

'It doesn't matter,' I lied, shaking my head. 'It happened a long time ago and I think my friend's left home now. I was just wondering about stories and stuff.'

'And she's OK?' Miranda turned her back on me.

No, I wanted to shout, but Miranda was back fiddling with her hair and besides I wasn't sure if I could trust the words any more. We were quiet then until she finished. I sang along with Bryan about how horrible it was to be jealous under my breath but I was finding it difficult to breathe. Was it safe to really leave the story there?

'So what do you think?' At last Miranda put down the straighteners and let her flattened hair swing from side to side.

'Everyone's going to get out of your way,' I said and then we laughed and it all seemed so normal that I let out a deep sigh which made Miranda smile again.

'Time to go now.' She bustled round the salon turning off lights and putting the equipment and brushes away. She switched off the music system and waited at the door for me to leave first so she could set the alarm. We kissed each other goodbye in the street. One cheek, two cheek, we hesitated over three before leaving it. 'I'll do your hair next time,' Miranda said. 'It'll look just darling.' But then instead of clitter-clattering down the street on those silly high heels she wore that made her look like an elephant on stilts, she held on to my arm tightly.

'Tell your friend to find a whole lot of made-up stories from somewhere else and pretend they happened to her,' she said. 'That way no one gets hurt.'

'Maybe.' I wanted to believe Miranda.

'I've got shelf-loads of love stories you can borrow if you want. It's all in there.'

'I didn't know you were a reader.'

'I didn't always want to be a hairdresser.' Miranda shook her head so her hair really did flare out, just like it did in her magazine pictures. 'That English teacher I told you about. He's got a lot to answer for.'

I bared my teeth, trying to smile along with her.

'And are you really sure you're all right?' she said.

I nodded, blinking the tears back. This was how to be normal. To learn when to be quiet. There was no reason why I couldn't do it. Not every story has to have an ending.

She looked at her watch and then grimaced. 'I must be off. Mum's got bingo tonight and I promised I'd look after Dad so she can enjoy a night off. He can't get around by himself, you know, not since his accident. Mind you, you'd be surprised at the trouble he can get up to in his wheelchair. Speedy, that's what Mum says we should call him.' She grimaced and then shook herself. 'You take care now, honey-girl. Time for me to love you and leave you. Don't do anything I wouldn't do,' she said brightly, her hair slicing the air around her as she walked away.

'Oh you,' I cooed as I stood looking at myself in my mirror. I lifted my skirt above my knees, looking at my legs harshly. I couldn't even pretend they were romantic tonight. They looked fat. Filled up with lies and unsaid things. Mr Roberts was right. The whole of me was nothing more than lumpy, mashed potatoes.

I shook myself all over in the mirror. My head, my arms, my bottom, my legs. I watched the fat wobble, wanting to prove to myself I wasn't as flabbily solid as Miranda. That my outline could be redrawn, even my bones broken.

And that was something I had to believe. That little chance of transformation. Otherwise what was the point of anything?

EIGHT

'I used to be a little scrap of a thing, so small no one really paid any attention to me.' I ignored Mr Roberts's snort from the bottom of the ladder as I noticed my voice turn to almost a whisper. 'Then all of a sudden one morning I woke up and it was as if I'd turned into someone else. With a cartoon sexy body I couldn't control. I can't have developed that quickly, of course, but it was what it felt like. None of my clothes fitted and at first Dad refused to waste money on new ones. I got to hate the way he'd glare at me every morning and tell me to pull my skirt down, or button up my shirt properly as if it were my fault I was popping out of everything. He was always on at me.

'I'd walk around with my arms crossed, my shoulders hunched, but you can't be on guard all the time. Round about that time, all the boys at school started to notice me too,' I spoke down to Mr Roberts. 'Even the little boys had crushes on me. Once when they had an exam, they begged me to give them a good luck kiss, queuing up so I wouldn't miss one out. They'd bring me presents, things they'd stolen from their mothers just so I'd remember them the next time I walked past.'

'What's that?' Mr Roberts grumbled. 'Speak up, Molly. You're mumbling.'

'But it was the boys my age who were the worst.' There was no one else in the shop but my heart was knocking against my chest so hard I could almost feel it vibrate against the shelf. 'My pigeon hole would be filled with notes. I'd find telephone numbers scribbled on my class books. They came round to my house in gangs and just stood outside the door. Once a boy knocked himself out on a lamppost because he was clowning around to get my attention. He had a black eye the next day at school.'

'Teenage boys,' Mr Roberts sighed. 'Too many hormones. They never learn.'

'But I wouldn't go near any of them,' I said. 'I think that's probably why they all kept after me. It wasn't that I didn't want a boyfriend. My father would never have let me. He thought it was all my fault.'

'Only natural to want to protect you,' Mr Roberts said.

'After that, nothing I did was right. I couldn't stop making him angry,' I said. 'I'd come out after school, and there he'd be, waiting for me. He'd glower at every boy who passed us when we walked home. He said he couldn't trust me. As if it were my fault.

'I learnt never to talk to boys anywhere, inside or outside school. And then not to girls either. He'd always find out somehow and there would be an inquisition. He made me wear all these really frumpy clothes. Once when we were at the shops, he had to leave me alone for a minute and a boy I'd never seen before came up and asked if I knew where the chemist was. That was all, but my father caught us and the fireworks went on for days.'

'Sounds a bit harsh,' Mr Roberts admitted. 'Although you do have to look after daughters.' He seemed unsure though and there was a silence before he spoke again. This time he was more enthusiastic. 'But did you meet the boy again?' he asked. 'The one in the shopping centre? Did you get up to some rumpus-pumpus? I bet you did, Molly. I know your sort. You like your hanky-panky. Nothing wrong with that.'

I squeezed my eyes shut and pictured the rage on my father's face as he came out of the gents to see me pointing to the bottom tier of the shopping centre and the boy nodding away. I'd just taken his rage for granted then, something I'd learnt to live with, but now I tried to see it through his eyes. What did he think could happen to make him so angry?

'We did,' I said. 'But not after. That same day. I got my father to leave me for five minutes by pretending I was buying him something special as an apology, and then I ran downstairs and met the boy. We went down one of those side corridors no one uses.'

'Just like that? In the shopping centre?' Mr Roberts whistled through his teeth. 'Weren't you worried someone would see you?'

'We were like animals,' I said.

'You dirty girl. It's unbelievable.' Mr Roberts held the ladder steady for me to come down.

'It's all true.' After all, my father had thought it was the truth. He probably pictured the whole scene in much more detail than I'd just told it.

'And not very nice,' Mr Roberts said, with more than a hint of pleasure.

He was right. It wasn't nice, but that night, for the first time since I could remember, I slept like a baby. I woke up early to the electric whinny of the milk van as it made deliveries along the High Street, and drifted back to the kind of safe half-sleep world where everything is sweet, anything is possible. I knew I had found my stories.

Maybe because I had already confessed to Miranda, it was easier to tell Mr Roberts I'd got a boyfriend.

I was halfway up the ladder, moving boxes of staplers and ballpoint pens from one side of the shelf to the other. Mr Roberts's hands were on my calves to keep me steady.

'I've got a boyfriend, you know,' I said. 'A proper one.' I paused a moment, waiting for his reaction.

'Well, good for you, girl. I knew you would get cleaned up, although—' He shook his head, his middle fingertip pressing against my flesh a little too hard.

'I'll still tell you stuff,' I said quickly. 'Maybe I can even tell you about Tim. It's OK. He won't mind.' He won't know, I whispered to myself.

'I'm not sure it will be the same,' Mr Roberts said. 'It seems impure somehow. Young love and all that.'

I held my breath because I knew I couldn't afford to lose my home and salary. Mr Roberts was quite capable of docking my wages if I didn't come up with the goods. I'd seen him with salesmen. They thought he was going to be an easy catch because of his woolly jumpers and funny thick glasses, but more often than not, they'd stand outside the shop afterwards, going over figures on their calculators as if they couldn't believe what had just happened to them.

If Mr Roberts spoke before I counted to ten then everything would be OK.

He came in exactly as I reached eight. 'We'll maybe see how it goes. Give it a few weeks.'

I shoved the box I'd been pretending to move right over to the end of the shelf. 'That's it finished up here,' I said cheerfully, but Mr Roberts kept his hand on my leg longer than he normally did. And he stayed where he was as I climbed down so I had to hold my body against his until I got to the bottom and could step aside. This was a new development, one I wasn't too sure about.

NINE

I watched Tim's hand brush along the back of the Seize the Day bench as if he was testing the grain of the wood. Then he made a sudden lunge, missing first and knocking my arm before finally taking my hand in his.

I squeezed back but then he started to hurt me so I tried to loosen his grasp. He shook his head and kept on pinching at my fingers. We carried on grasping each other in silence although I could see my skin turning white.

'I've been plucking up the courage to ask you something,' he said eventually.

'Go on,' I encouraged. I felt so light when I was with him. So free of any need to be looking over my shoulder.

'I was wondering if I might kiss you tomorrow,' he said.

I burst out laughing. I couldn't help it. 'You can kiss me now.' I pouted my lips out to him.

'No,' he said. 'I would prefer it to be tomorrow.'

Knowing I was going to be kissed made me jumpy and restless the next day. I couldn't eat anything, not even my usual breakfast of a fruit scone. It was still sitting in its brown paper bag under the till at lunchtime.

In the end, I went over to persuade Miranda to take an extra cigarette break because Mr Roberts wasn't helping my mood. He had already made me do all sorts of unnecessary chores around the shop that morning, shifting the display of envelopes from one side of the room to the other, telling me to go up and interrupt customers who were happily browsing and ask if they wanted something, making me sort out the coloured pencils into separate jars. He was watching me for signs of love, he said. We couldn't afford to let things get slipshod just because cupid had shot his arrow.

At last a big order from the Insurance Office on Silver Street came in, and as he never trusted me with anything important, he bustled round ticking things off the list. This gave me a small respite.

Miranda and I huddled in the doorway of the fashion boutique next to her salon. Despite the fact that the two women who ran it were arrow-thin, continually pointing themselves in successful directions, they never opened their shop before eleven in the morning, so it was a useful place for us to meet.

'There's this little girl been born somewhere who's got a bottom half like a tail,' Miranda told me. 'Both legs are joined together and they're going to have to do an operation to separate them. There was an interview with the doctor in my magazine. They called him Dr Mermaid, because that's what the girl looks like. Apparently the operation rarely works but he never gives up hope.'

'How do you practise kissing?' I interrupted her.

'You must have kissed someone,' she said, surprised.

'Of course I have, stupid,' I lied. 'But I want this to be perfect. I'm sure there used to be a way the girls at school rehearsed.'

'With a banana,' Miranda said firmly. 'You snog a banana.'

It was only after I'd nipped across to the supermarket and got myself a whole bunch of bananas that weren't even on special offer that Miranda came into the shop and said she'd just remembered she'd got it wrong. Bananas weren't for practising kissing. They were for something altogether different. And had I heard about this woman who went into a supermarket in Manchester and had been bitten by a tarantula who came over on a bunch of bananas?

That night, on the Seize the Day bench, Tim made to take my hand before he stopped and asked me to shut my eyes. I did and then held my hand out, open fingered, to him. My arm was shaking, but instead of holding on to me, pulling me closer as I hoped, I felt him slipping something egg shaped into my palm.

I opened my eyes and peered down. A walnut was cupped there, looking withered and brain-like.

'What's this?' I asked.

'Shhhh.' Tim looked round. 'You have to learn to speak quieter, Molly. Trees have ears.'

'Sorry,' I whispered. 'But why've you given me a nut?'

'It contains a secret. A word only you will know.'

I stared at him. He looked completely serious. His brows were too heavy for the thinness of his face. They overshadowed every other feature and made him look dangerous in the wrong lights.

'How will I know I've got the right word?' I asked.

'Hold it. Think.'

So I did. I shut my eyes again and the word came. It came miraculously. I knew it was right without questioning. I just didn't know what it meant in this context.

'Fridge,' I said, and when I opened my eyes, Tim was smiling, not at me but I knew it was because of me. I was so proud it felt like a ball of sunshine had burst in my stomach.

'And now I'll kiss you,' he said.

There are kisses and kisses. Prostitutes never kiss. Most teenagers dream of doing nothing else. The sound of a mother's kiss was taken up in a spaceship to soothe aliens on distant planets. Eskimos kiss by rubbing noses. To kiss Marilyn Monroe was apparently like kissing Hitler so bristly was her upper lip. To kiss at the point of ejaculation guarantees a child genius. So complicated is social kissing that it's safer for normal people like Miranda and myself just to stand there, waiting for one, or two, or even three cheeks to be airbrushed towards us. French kisses. Butterfly kisses. Kissing cousins. Kiss of life. Kiss of death.

Tim's kiss was a lick of melon.

Honey sweet melon fresh in your mouth at breakfast time when you're on holiday and life is good. In fact it's never been better.

I put my hand up to my mouth when he finally drew away. I rubbed the tips of my fingers over my lips. It was a good job I was sitting down because my legs were shaky. It was as if Tim had sucked all the air from my body.

So this was what it was all about.

'Do you think we could do that again?' I asked.

He took the walnut from me. I hadn't realised I'd been holding it so tightly until I felt him prise my fingers open one by one to release it.

'No.' He shook his head. He'd stopped smiling now. 'But tomorrow we can.'

I must have sighed then, because Tim took my hand and rubbed the dent that was still on my palm from where I'd been clutching the walnut.

'If we're spared,' he added.

TEN

The day after the Kiss was late night shopping for the posh end of town.

Down on our side of the street though, we closed at five sharp every night. Sometimes Mr Roberts and I would get customers who'd come and press their noses at the door and rattle the handle, confused as to why they could buy designer shoes or fancy jewellery at eight o'clock at night, but not a box file or a pencil.

'Because we've got bloody homes to go to, mate,' Mr Roberts would mouth at them, and I'd nod along with the righteous warmth of being on the inside although, of course, I didn't exactly have a home to rush back to.

I went to the bench instead, and Tim was waiting for me, hunched up inside his jumper. He pulled the sleeves down to cover his hands. A red scarf was wrapped tightly round his neck.

'It's a bit chilly,' he said, and then he stood up, took my hand and told me to trust him. I could almost feel the energy coming off him as he pulled me down half-lit alleys I'd never noticed before, through car parks and shop yards. Waiters looked up at us as they sat on the back steps of their restaurants, sipping coffee and having cigarettes before the evening rush began. An older man and young woman embraced just behind a half-open office door, his briefcase slotted between their legs.

Tim didn't say a word even as we passed through the automatic doors of the shopping centre. He'd been hushing me all the way along as I tried to make conversation. We stood there for a moment, breathing in the smell of freshly baked bread from the café at the entrance.

'It's not real, that smell,' I rambled. 'It's a spray they use, or they put it in the air conditioning. It was in one of Miranda's magazines. A woman once seriously hurt herself by . . .' I had to put my hand over my mouth to shut myself up.

Tim pulled me along again. In the town's one department store, he led the way up to home furnishings, going not by the lift or even the escalator, but through an unmarked door and up by the staff steps.

'Are we allowed?' I asked, but he didn't hesitate once, not even when we passed a uniformed security guard coming down carrying three heavy boxes. Then through another door and we were back in the main part of the shop. We were standing in front of a display case full of glass ornaments when he turned to me.

'Have you seen anything more beautiful?' he said.

He pointed at a statue of a polar bear, about six inches high, framed in a square box. The bear was made of clear white glass apart from its four cloudy legs and it had an etched expression of tranquillity on its face. The base was spiked up to look like falling snow. The rim of the box was edged with gold. Inside, the bear had a curious wild dignity amongst the sparkly bejewelled cats and dogs it kept company with on the shelves.

We stood on either side of it. When I bent down to the bear's level, I looked right through it and saw Tim staring just as intensely from the other side. But then he caught me looking at him and started to laugh. His smile was warm and real through the icy perfection of the glass. I felt something melt inside me as I laughed back.

'It's trapped,' he said. 'I come and look at it sometimes to work out how I can help it break free.'

'Can't you just buy it?' I asked. 'Or steal it.'

Tim shook his head. 'That would just be forcing it into another kind of captivity,' he said. 'It would be under an obligation then.'

'It's very beautiful,' I said, because it was. I didn't tell Tim I disagreed with him. There was a feeling of calmness about the bear that made me think it was exactly where it wanted to be.

'Come on, Molly,' he said. 'Let's get ourselves home.'

'Home?' I asked.

He looked surprised. 'To the bench,' he said. 'Where else?'

'I didn't really mix with the girls at school,' I told Mr Roberts from the top of my ladder, 'but there was one girl, Leanne, who I liked. She spent a lot of time on her own too.'

The ladder shuddered as Mr Roberts coughed. 'Sorry, Molly,' he said. 'Just not been feeling too good recently. Mrs Roberts keeps on at me to go to the doctor's.' He coughed again.

I shut my eyes until he'd finished. 'You were never really allowed to stay in the school buildings at break-time,' I said. 'They had this idea that fresh air was good for you, but what it meant was that everyone congregated in bits of the playground where you couldn't be seen and there they'd smoke or get up to other trouble. Sometimes they'd even creep through the trees and go into town. The older ones went to the pub.'

'Did you?'

'Wouldn't have been worth the risk of my father catching me. Instead I begged this biology teacher to let me stay inside. I said I was frightened about being bullied, and to my surprise she believed me. She let me stay in the detention room and while the other students were getting on with the punishments they'd been set, I'd sit there staring into space. The funny thing was that it got me the reputation for being a real hard case because all the other kids thought I wasn't bothering to do the extra work. I didn't mind. It just meant people left me even more alone.'

'And that's where you met Leanne?'

'Yep. She was often there too. We never really talked but one day as she was leaving, she slipped something onto my desk. I was about to call out after her when I looked at it. It was a lipstick in a shiny silver case. When I opened it up I could see it was bright red.

'Of course when I got home, I couldn't resist trying the lipstick on in front of the mirror. It made me look older, harder, the kind of girl who wouldn't be bothered what her father thought. I pulled a chair over to the window and stared at the people passing by in the street, hoping they would look up at me and see this mysterious, beautiful woman and wonder about me. I can't have been more than about fourteen.'

I could tell by the trembling of the ladder that Mr Roberts was laughing below.

'Anyway I was so wrapped up in this daydream that I didn't hear my father's footsteps outside the room. He stormed in, almost pulling the door handle off he was so angry.

'"What the hell do you think you're doing?" he yelled. "I come home tired from work, take one look up at my own house and what do I see but you sitting there half-dressed like a prostitute in Amsterdam. Clean that muck off your face straight away."'

'Were you half-dressed?' Mr Roberts asked.

I'd been wearing my school uniform. My hair was tied up tightly in two plaits. I didn't even know at that time what a prostitute in Amsterdam looked like. I had to research it in the encyclopaedia at the school library.

'Molly, were you half-dressed?' Mr Roberts's voice jolted me back to the present.

'Yes,' I said. 'I'd stripped down to my undies. I was leaning forward so the men passing by could see all of me. Every so often

I'd lift my leg and pretend to scratch it so I could stretch it out again, give them a better look. There were about five men standing outside the window watching me. I liked it. I liked them watching me. I put on a show. I promised them that I'd be there the next day too.'

Mr Roberts tut-tutted with delight.

'I think I've finished up here now,' I said, shoving one of the boxes to the side. I pulled my skirt tight around my knees as I climbed down, smoothing it straight with my palms when I reached the safety of the shop floor.

ELEVEN

'Tim,' I said, hours later as we sat entwined on the park bench. 'Why do we never talk?'

'Hmmm . . . ?' His foot stopped tapping on the grass. He lifted his chin up so he could look at me. 'We're always talking,' he said.

'We're not. I don't mind. I just wonder if we should do a bit more sometimes. Maybe we could go to the pub or something.'

'Come with me.' He stood up and held out his hand to help me up. I started to walk automatically towards the centre of the park where the paths were brightly lit and clearly marked, but Tim had other ideas. 'Not that way!' he said.

Instead he took me into the bushes that edged the park, holding down branches for me to climb over, catching prickly twigs so they didn't tear my clothes. I followed him, complaining.

'Shhhh.' He put a finger over my lips. We were standing against a house wall that backed on to the park. 'Put your ear to the wall. Can you hear anything?'

I shook my head.

Tim frowned. 'Come this way,' he said. I followed Tim again round to one of the cul-de-sacs running off the park. 'Stare in the window as you walk past. Not too obviously, but take a close look.'

A woman was sitting on the sofa talking on the telephone. She was twisting a lock of hair round and round a finger, laughing and speaking into the receiver.

'And now come back and listen properly,' he whispered and I

made my way back. 'Put your head really tight against the wall.'

I still couldn't hear anything but the bricks felt warmer against my cheek. I nodded at Tim, pretending it was working and he looked pleased.

'I listen to her a lot,' he said. 'She's one of my favourites. I call her the happy woman. But they're everywhere, Molly. Think about it. You don't even have to go against the wall once you become expert. People speak into the phone and someone miles away hears their voice, but what they don't realise is the hundreds of other people those noise waves have to go through in order to get to the right one. All those other words they've picked up on the way. That's why we're always talking. You just have to train yourself to listen.'

It made sense. That was the stupid thing. What Tim had just said made perfect sense. Before I followed him back, I put my ear back against the wall. I could swear I heard a giggle and then a series of random words – horse, field, bikini – prickling through my skin. It was as if I was joining in the conversation, a dowsing wand between both speaker and listener.

Tim and I fought our way back through the undergrowth in silence until we reached the bench. And then as I was about to say something about his theory or just say anything because I wanted it to be only our words we heard between us, he kissed me.

The next night in Miranda's hair salon, Edith Piaf seemed to be the only person regretting nothing as Miranda cursed under her breath. She was struggling to perfect her back-combing technique on my hair and things weren't going well. She'd already snapped at me for eating Smarties while she worked.

'Your hair's too thin,' she complained. 'I don't think this is going to work. It's not falling out, is it? I'm sure it was thicker than this last time.'

She kept peering across my shoulder at the magazine clipping she'd Sellotaped on the salon mirror. It was of a woman walking along a beach with two small dogs yapping at her heels.

'You can't even see what her hair looks like,' I pointed out. 'And why is it my fault anyway?'

'It's the general spirit I'm after,' she said. 'All that just got out of bed stuff and hungry eyes they're always going on about.' She brushed my hair in angry up and down movements until I could swear it was starting to crackle under the strain.

I looked at my reflection, more unkempt witch than tousled pillow, before putting my fingers up to trace the outline of my lips. They seemed fuller somehow. Redder. A great big sign of how often I was being kissed. Tim and I still hadn't gone further although I kept my eyes shut often now, as he preferred, and leant against him more with my whole weight, hoping he'd take the hint that I wouldn't really mind if he wanted to do a bit more. I closed my eyes now, feeling a tremor run through me.

'Now what's wrong with you?'

I jolted up as Miranda prodded me painfully on my shoulder.

'You're looking a bit peewally, if you don't mind me saying,' she said. 'Do you want me to walk you home?'

'No.' I'd managed to keep Miranda out of my room so far, just giving her the general impression that I was in some kind of flat, with bathroom and mini-kitchen. I didn't want any horror she might feel at my lack of home comforts to spoil my satisfaction at this life I was carving out for myself. I tried to change the subject. 'So who is this woman you're torturing me into looking like anyway?'

'Oh Molly, you're not telling me you don't know who this is?'

I couldn't help but laugh when I saw Miranda's expression. She was genuinely shocked.

'Now that's only Brigitte Bardot,' she said. 'The original sex goddess.'

'Her?' I peeled the photograph of the mirror so I could look at it closer. 'She's a bit old.'

'Well she is now, silly. The life she's led though, it makes your heart bleed. I'll tell you the whole story one day. And of course she's gone all animal mad as those sort of women always do when they lose their looks. But she was beautiful once.'

'And French?' I was getting to know Miranda.

'Of course.' Miranda smiled at me in the mirror. 'I've got better photographs of her at home, walking along in St Tropez, barefoot, all these men staring at her.'

'I've heard of Saint Wotzername,' I said. I picked out a red Smartie from the tube and started rubbing it round my lips, smacking them together in the mirror to see the colour.

'St Tropez,' Miranda purred. 'That could be us, Molly. Strolling hand in hand with dark Frenchmen before we take champagne on one of the yachts there. They'd buy us pearls to wind round our necks, diamonds for our fingers. Tiaras even. They'd feed us with their fingers, the tastiest piece of lobster, an oyster straight from the shell.'

'I get a bit seasick on water,' I warned. 'My tiara would probably drop off as I was vomiting over the edge of the yacht.'

'We'd go to nightclubs until morning, dancing and drinking cocktails.' Miranda ignored me. 'Walk home in our glittery evening dresses, smiling at all the ordinary people we passed as they rush off to work. Just imagine.'

'And who exactly would pay for all our dresses?'

But when Miranda didn't answer and I looked at her reflection, I saw it was her turn to shut her eyes and feel that tremor. She was even leaning against the chair with her whole weight, her head softly falling to one side. The only clue that she was still alive was the way her lips moved to mime along with the French words coming from the CD player. I picked the photograph up from the counter and turned it over and over in my hands, waiting for Miranda to come back down to earth and finish the hairdo.

TWELVE

It was partly because of that heavy-eyed look of Miranda's and the fact that Tim hadn't been in the park for a few days that I went looking in the library for some of the love stories Miranda had told me about. I wasn't expecting much.

Certainly not to fall in love myself. Not in the library anyway. But there she was – my first proper crush on a French woman – nestling between Jonathan Coe and a misplaced George Eliot. I'd just been running my fingers over the spines of the books hoping for one to jump out at me. It was the single name that attracted me first. That, and the old-fashioned orange colour of her book. I pulled it out and turned to the back, as I usually did, to have a look at the writer's photograph before I decided to bother with the story.

Colette had a long, varied and active life.

It was looking good.

At the age of twenty she had plunged herself into a different world…

Love at first read. By sheer luck, I'd picked on someone who understood the advantages of reinvention. Maybe I could even learn something from her.

'Feathery near-pornography,' read the quote on the back of the book. Perfect. It might be perfect for stories for Mr Roberts too. I took it straight to the desk and joined the queue. The man in front of me wanted to know where he could obtain proper back-copies of the *Daily Telegraph*. He twiddled his moustache as he shouted how he didn't want to have to read them on microfiche, the stories weren't the same on computer.

'But they're exactly the same words,' said the librarian patiently, but the man hee-hawed in her face.

'If God meant us to use computers, He'd have given us television aerials on the top of our heads. This is a library. For the *written* word. For which our God gave us *eyes*,' he said, looking for all the world as if he'd scored not just one point over her, but won the whole war.

She stared at him so fiercely though, he backed away.

'In my day, sentences were meant to be treasured,' he said in a weak parting shot. 'Not computered out of all existence. And I would expect you of all people to understand that!'

The librarian merely looked past him to smile at me, but I was torn. Instinct and training meant I wanted to be the good girl for her because she was Authority, but I hated computers too. I compromised by trying to look as if I hadn't heard anything.

'Ooh Colette,' she purred as she stamped my book. 'How nice. And how unusual to see someone young enjoying a forgotten writer. Have you read her biography?'

I shook my head.

'It's super,' she said. 'You really must, but then again maybe it's only when you get to my age that you prefer real life over fiction.'

As I left the library, the *Daily Telegraph* man was standing there, looking at the notice board in the entrance hall.

'I liked what you said about having an aerial in your head,' I said, but I must have been too quiet because he didn't seem to hear me, just kept staring up at the mixture of handwritten cards and brightly coloured posters.

'Goodbye then,' I said, pausing a minute but he didn't as much as turn round. I pinched myself hard on the thigh as I walked home clutching the book with my other hand so it wouldn't fly away with all its feathery near-pornography.

I did exist. Pinch, pinch. I did exist.

THIRTEEN

Tim and I spent the evening pushing each other on the swings.

'Did you have a happy childhood?' I asked.

'It was OK.' It was my turn to push him. He had his head back so he was looking straight up at the sky. He was moving too quickly now for me to get hold of him properly so I just stood there behind him, watching his face loom in and out of sight. 'You're an upside down Molly,' he laughed, finally slowing down.

'Aren't you going to ask me?' I said, sitting down on the next swing. I tried to wind the ropes together so we were entwined, but they kept springing loose.

'If you want me to.'

I thought about this. Tim was swinging faster again, pushing his legs up and down to speed himself up, so I started swinging myself.

'I'm flying,' I shouted, and then for several wonderful moments Tim and I were swinging in perfect synchronicity. I pushed my head right back, letting my hair fall down and watched the stars. It was as if they were all shooting in different directions.

Later as we walked back to the bench, Tim put his hand out to stroke my hair. 'Beautiful,' he said.

'You need to ask me things because you want to know the answer, not because I ask you to,' I said. 'That's the only way we're going to find out about each other.' I was still annoyed about his earlier lack of interest in my childhood.

'But I know you already,' he said. 'It's my job to know things like that. You're Molly. Beautiful inside and out. What more do I need to know?'

I was quiet then. Too busy thinking.

Mr Roberts was breathing heavily below me as once more I shifted the stationery boxes from one side of the shelf to the other.

'Remember I told you about Leanne,' I said. 'The one that gave me the red lipstick?'

'The naughty one,' Mr Roberts said.

'She was different from the rest of us. We were tough country girls but she was like a town mouse, a timid little thing with these big eyes and a gentle voice. She needed looking after, but there was something about her that made me want to crush her and just stroke her hair, both at the same time. It's hard to explain.'

Now I'd got into the flow, the story was telling itself.

'She started to bring me other things too. Nothing you'd bother about too much. A bit like her, really. Once she stood very close to me when she handed me a hairclip, and she smelt of lemons,' I continued. 'Lemons, clean white shirts and sun-kissed skin. I had to close my eyes it was that powerful. I was leaning into her without realising, wanting to inhale her, to touch her. It was like she was a window out to somewhere else. But the poor little thing was frightened of everything, so when this gang of boys came down the corridor she got scared. She put her hand into mine, as if I could look after her, although we were the same age. Mind you, I was probably double her size, even then.

'It was like holding a heart in my hand, her little fingers curling up into mine. We stayed frozen like that, even when the bell went for the end of break. It was only when everyone had gone into class, and it was just us two left in the corridor, we realised we were still holding hands. I didn't want to let her go.'

'So what did you do?'

I'd forgotten about Mr Roberts. I was picturing what it must have felt like, holding on to Leanne's hand. You know when you catch a bird and you can feel its heart beating almost out of its body. You realise how fragile that life-force is. How little it would take to stop it.

'I kissed her,' I said. 'We kissed each other very gently, and then slowly the tip of my tongue went out and licked round her lips. She parted her teeth with this little gasp and I traced their edges with my tongue. She was like a boy, shape-wise, so we fitted together, but she didn't taste like a boy. She tasted like fruit. Fresh fruit.' I thought of how Tim had tasted of melon. 'There was nothing bad about her.'

Was it my imagination or was the ladder shaking a little now? I shut my eyes to try to concentrate on the scene I was describing.

'And her skin didn't feel like a boy's either. Or at least not that bit of her neck underneath her hair, when I pulled it up to kiss her there too. It was so soft, like the underbelly of a kitten. I stroked her shoulders through her thin cotton shirt. She held on to my waist.' I wasn't sure which were my words any more. All I wanted was that feeling of salty sweetness that I'd got when I was reading Colette. 'We cleaved together,' I said finally.

I was trying to smell the school corridor, the scent of disinfectant, wax crayons and sweat. But there was something I'd been missing.

'She was French,' I said suddenly.

Mr Roberts gasped below me. 'You've never said that before,' he said.

'Why should I? And that's all I going to tell you this time too,' I said, looking back down at him. 'Now if you'll just get out of my way, I'd better get on with stuff in the shop.'

And he did get out of my way. This time he jumped to the side,

Sarah Salway

while still holding the ladder steady. It made me want to laugh but I didn't. I practised my tragically fragile smile instead, the one where I felt wistful for all the dreadful things that had happened to me but still looked forward, bravely, to a bright future.

FOURTEEN

Miranda wasn't my only friend any more.

On my second visit to the library, I'd plucked up the courage to ask Liz, the librarian, which were the best books about love. She looked at me strangely and then took me over to a shelf on which there were lots of brightly coloured books with cartoon women on their covers. After I'd been flicking through them aimlessly, she came back.

'Not what you want?' she asked.

I shook my head. 'I used to love Charlotte Brontë at school,' I said. 'I was just looking for something a bit different. I suppose I'll just stick with Colette.'

'Come and see me next time,' she said, 'and I'll find something different for you.'

So the next time I went to the library, Liz was waiting. She let me sit with her in the kitchen during her coffee break before handing over a handwritten list of books she said she thought I might enjoy.

'This is what we should have learnt at school,' I said, trying to sound as eager as I could as I read through the list. It was full of French sounding names I'd never heard of before. 'This is what matters. I want to know everything about love, not maths or history.'

I took another of the chocolate biscuits Liz had put out on a plate for me although she wouldn't eat one herself. 'A moment on the lips,' she said.

After that, whenever Liz wasn't on her breaks, I'd go and sit on one of the comfortable low chairs in the fiction section. While I read, Liz would come and sort out books beside me, whispering gossip as she clicked authors alphabetically into their slots. She treated dead and living writers, fictional characters and library users in exactly the same way.

'Of course, Anaïs Nin was a bigamist before she died,' she told me once. 'And do you know that once one husband rang the other, but Anaïs passed him off as a madman. He probably believed her because she was beautiful, but they used to say too that the Duchess of Devonshire had skin that was so fresh it sparkled. People would bring chairs to the park especially so they could stand on them to see her when she went past. And talking of chairs, that Karen Cooper with the little baby was in the library yesterday. Not much older than you but her skin was so red and blotchy I couldn't really look at her, and her boobs were hanging out of her T-shirt. Some people should study themselves in the mirror with a bit more care. Oh, but talking of boobs, do listen to this. When Rimbaud's body was carried down the street for his funeral, the prostitutes of Paris all lifted up their tops to show his coffin their bare breasts as a tribute to their own wild child. Isn't that killing?'

It was. So killing I'd stopped trying to keep up with her but it was still hard to get my breath back so I could concentrate on my book.

'So have you got a boyfriend?' she asked.

'I have,' I said. 'He's called Tim.' It wasn't hard at all to say this any more. In fact, it was nice to have someone to talk to about him. I hadn't mentioned him to Miranda since she asked if he was 'all right up there' when I said about how he'd taught me to listen through walls, and Mr Roberts was too fixated on Leanne nowadays to want to talk about anyone else.

Liz sighed. 'And is he lovely?' she laughed. 'Does he make your heart go pitter-patter?'

'He does. He's, oh Liz, he's everything nice.'

'They always are at first,' Liz said. 'It's keeping them that way that's the problem. Still, if there wasn't heartbreak in the world then there wouldn't be books. And then where would we be, Molly?'

Here, I wanted to say. Still right here.

And for once, it wasn't a bad place to be.

'Mind you, I shouldn't be raining on your parade.' Liz slotted a book back in its place so hard the whole shelf trembled. 'Maybe you've got the one good one. God knows he must be out there, otherwise what's the point of all this?' She gestured at the books lining the room.

I watched her carefully as she reached up to put another book back. The fat on her upper arms wobbled until it looked as if it was taking on a life of its own. I couldn't imagine Liz outside the library. She was like most of the books here, unread and slightly dusty, but as she slotted the next book back just as violently as she had the last, I thought how that wasn't fair. There amongst all the plots, I was starting to hatch one of my own.

FIFTEEN

'Tell me more about the little French girl,' Mr Roberts begged. This was the third time in as many days.

I stared at him until he reached into the till and picked out another ten pound note. I put it quickly in my jeans pocket.

'We used to go down to this field after school,' I told Mr Roberts. 'We were feral children. I had this long curly hair I could never keep tied in a bow, but Leanne was always neater than me. Her hair was thin and blonde, and she kept it short. Once she fell into the stream and we didn't have a towel or anything so I dried her feet with my hair, wrapped it round and round her toes.

'She was shaking, just gently but still shaking. Like a lamb when you catch it.'

'Lambs don't shake,' Mr Roberts said. 'They jump.'

I looked down at him sharply. I was trying to establish a rule that he was to keep silent during my storytelling. Every time he started to interrupt or to take over the story in any way, I'd stop. He might be in charge of the shop, but the ladder had become my territory.

'Go on. Please,' he pleaded, and I decided to be merciful this time.

'And then because my face was down there,' I said, 'I licked between her big toe and the next very gently. It was wet from the stream, but I could taste her salty skin underneath. She hid her face in her petticoat so when I looked up all I could see was this frothy white lace, but I knew she liked it.'

Mr Roberts moaned, but said nothing. He was proving surprisingly easy to train.

The strange thing was that it wasn't just the money that made me tell the stories. Because if Leanne could turn out to be French and desirable, then lots of other things around me could shift too. I started watching other girls my age and I'd feel sorry for them. They couldn't see that the young man with the older woman they were giggling about was a gigolo. The old woman was an elderly courtesan having her last romantic fling. He didn't love her, and she didn't love him, but they both pretended until one day they woke up and found it was true. But neither could confess and they went their separate ways, living out the rest of their lives wondering what might have been if they'd been able to be truthful.

I'd wake up in my little bare room above the stationery shop, dreaming I was in Paris, in a luxurious boudoir above the park, sleeping in a gold barred bed between clean white cotton sheets, and that an elderly but loving servant was downstairs making me hot chocolate with fresh bread for breakfast. There were times I could even smell the bread baking.

What I was doing, the way I was living, stopped being a space in which I merely existed and became instead the wild gypsy-like existence I'd always dreamt of.

'Have I told you about the time Leanne and I went to the seaside and ate rock?' I asked Mr Roberts, but he just groaned. 'I will tomorrow,' I promised, and I jumped as gracefully as I could from the ladder.

SIXTEEN

'No one comes from nowhere,' Miranda said. She was painting strands of my hair a tangerine colour and then wrapping them up in silver foil. The bright hot lights were turning my face red and I looked like a turkey.

Still, having my hair done, and staring in the mirror all that time, seemed part of the whole thing. I wanted all the scents, the mousses, the colours. All the stuff that other women took for granted. Sometimes when I hadn't managed to get to the leisure centre for a shower for some days, I'd smell my arm surreptitiously in the shop, enjoying the slight animal whiff of the skin against the apple-lemon mist that seemed to come permanently out of my hair these days.

I'd taken to drawing thick kohl lines around my eyes and plastering white powder on my cheeks so that I looked more like Colette did in the postcard that Liz had shown me. It wasn't a look Miranda approved of – 'why spoil the natural beauty of your little face with all that hippy stuff?' she asked – but Miranda did what no one had ever done for me before. She did what I asked her to do. And, although she grumbled when I asked her to tint my hair red, she eventually agreed.

Mind you, she wouldn't cut my hair short and perm it, not just yet. She seemed to think she had to take responsibility for me. Just one year older, and she felt *in loco parentis*.

'Perhaps you want to talk it over with someone first?' she asked. 'What does your mum think about your hair?'

'Nothing,' I said. 'It's my hair.'

She shook her head sadly, fixing me with a look that seemed to say she knew the answer to her next question. 'You must have someone who cares whether you're OK or not. My mum always likes to know what I'm up to.'

'You care enough about me for everyone,' I said. It was meant to be a joke, but it came out too seriously and Miranda looked surprised.

'That's different,' she said. She must have caught the expression on my face because she went on quickly. 'Although I do, of course. You know I do, petal. It's just that . . .'

'Just what?' I wasn't being difficult. I really couldn't see what Miranda was talking about. If I wasn't worried, why should she be?

'You can't rely on me, Molly,' Miranda said. 'It's not as if I'm family or anything. You shouldn't just put your trust in anyone.'

I laughed. 'You're better than any family,' I said. 'I could tell you things about my family that—'

'How about coming back with me and having your tea with us soon?' Miranda always interrupted me when I was about to tell her anything personal about the past. In some ways it was a relief. I wasn't sure I was ready to tell anyone everything just yet. Besides keeping silent meant I didn't have to sort the facts out just yet. Everything was still floating. 'Me and mum and dad,' Miranda continued. 'Get some real home cooking into you for a change.'

And then she started telling me about a woman she'd read about in one of her magazines who was trapped in a relationship with a man who force-fed her because he had a thing for fat people.

SEVENTEEN

Surprisingly for someone who never let himself get pinned down, Tim had a passion for routine and order.

One evening when I turned up half an hour late at the park, he was so angry he could barely talk to me at first. He apologised though, saying that discipline was an essential quality in his line of business.

'What's that?' I asked him.

'You'll be better off if you don't know,' he said.

'Go on, tell me.' I knew I was pestering him, but I couldn't believe I still didn't know what he did. It was clear he did something. And something interesting. Although he looked scruffy and Miranda would die a million deaths if she saw the state of his hair, there was definitely something busy and purposeful about him. I could see that he had money from the way he dressed. Even though he never wore socks, his shoes were made of that shiny leather that felt as soft as the surface of any ten pound note. He spoke poshly too, clipping the starts of his consonants and raising his voice at the end of sentences as if he wasn't giving orders, just expecting his wishes to be carried out automatically. He must have been a good five years older than me, and certain things he said made me think he'd gone to university. But, despite all this, he never talked about having a job.

'I'm an adviser,' he said eventually. 'I advise people.'

I waited for him to go on. 'Like a personal trainer in the gym?' I asked, although even I would admit that Tim was lacking in the six-pack department. Sure enough, he winced and shook his head. 'So what do you advise about exactly then, Tim, and who?' I asked.

'The trouble is,' he laced his hands together and cracked his finger knuckles hard, 'if I tell you any more, Molly, I'll have to kill you.'

He was joking, I knew that. He must have been, although he wasn't smiling. What surprised me though was my reaction. I didn't want to laugh at all. Rather I felt a tingle of excitement and a rush of joy. I wanted Tim to put his arms around me and hug me to him. I wanted everyone to look at us and see me with him.

'Shall we go for a walk?' I asked him. I was that desperate to show him off.

'Let's just stay here. Safer that way,' he said.

And so I told him the truth about Jessica. I told him everything I could remember from what I had been told about her, and what I'd picked up from seeing her around, little bits of her life and who she was. I spoke quietly, slowly, weighing each word so that none would be a lie. I said how some of us had been jealous after she died. I told him about the little clusters that had formed in the playground for days afterwards and how even I had joined in. We'd talked about doing the same thing, how death was, after all, the great adventure, and how, because Jessica was one of the cool girls, we thought that maybe suicide was going to become cool now too. It was a way out, I said. I think for most of us it was the first time we realised that there could be a way out.

Tim listened. 'So she was never really your friend?' he asked.

I thought of Miranda's advice about believing in something being more important than the truth and all the stories I'd stolen and made my own for Mr Roberts, and for a moment I was tempted. But Tim was different. I knew he was interested in whatever I said, regardless of what it said about me.

'No,' I admitted. 'I was invisible to her kind. She wouldn't have crossed the street to help me if I'd been run over by a one-legged, three-eyed monster driving a tractor.'

And suddenly, with that unexpected gust of joy similar to the one I was learning to love in Liz, lighting up his whole body in exactly the same way, Tim started to laugh. It started small but then it exploded all over him until I joined in too.

'A one-legged—,' he gasped for breath.

'Three-eyed—,' I tried to continue but my stomach was hurting from the laughter.

'And why the bloody tractor?' Tim wheezed. I was crying by this time but it felt so good to just tell the truth. I felt all cleared out. Fresh and ready to start all over again. Free.

We just sat there and held hands for a while after that. We watched the park darken in silence, although every so often I'd look across at him, or he'd look across at me, and we'd start laughing all over again. I'm so lucky, I thought. I must remember that this is how it feels to be a winner. I stroked the arm of the Seize the Day bench. It can be done, Jessica, I whispered. You can get things right. You don't always need a way out.

I stood up then and started to clear the ground around her bench, throwing everything carefully into the bin. 'I'm going to get this bin moved away from here,' I shouted across to Tim. He was walking round the tree opposite. He looked as if he was pacing, counting each step as he went. 'No one ever bothers to aim properly so there's always stuff left littered around. And do you know what, Tim?' He didn't reply. He was bent over, digging in the earth with his fingers now. 'I can't bear to think of a rubbish bin being the only thing Jessica has to nestle up next to, not when she's alone at night.'

I put my shoulder against it to see if I could shift it myself but the metal frame was stuck into a slab of concrete. 'Maybe if

I asked one of the park attendants they'd do it for me?' I said. 'I could even write a letter to the council if that doesn't work.'

Suddenly I realised it was the first time in months I had plans for something other than just my own survival. I felt full of purpose.

'You're good for me,' I called out to Tim, before going over to drape myself over his back. 'You're my very own special adviser.'

EIGHTEEN

There were times on top of Mr Roberts's ladder when I opened my mouth and surprised myself. I would be up there high above the shop, on my own personal tightrope, hanging on fast, telling my stories as quickly as I could just to stay upright. Whole spiels would come spiralling out from nowhere.

Look! I longed to shout. Molly's Amazing Acrobatics.

And not a safety net in sight.

Once as Mr Roberts and I whiled away a quiet hour on a rainy April afternoon, it turned out that Leanne's father, and I was as surprised as anyone about this, used to be a juggler. He met Leanne's mother when she was a ballerina, fallen on hard times in regional pantomime. Her parentage explained Leanne's smallness, but her strength too. After all, there'd been that time she hit me when she got jealous of me and the French teacher, Madame Gilligan. (The Madame had just popped out Colette-style.) I had grappled with Leanne and we ended up fighting in the middle of the gym while all the other girls and boys clapped us on. I tore her dress, she ripped the buttons off my blouse so my breasts were bare. Oh, we were wild girls.

'Wild girls,' Mr Roberts repeated. He always wanted to hear more about Leanne. He liked the way she taught me the tricks that would allow us one day to appear in the circus ring together, lessons she'd learnt at her daddy's knee.

'When are you going to show me that nude juggling trick with lit torches you learnt how to do so well,' he asked.

'Well, it's a bit of a fire risk to do it in a stationery shop when there's so much paper around, but one day soon,' I promised.

'She was a clever little girl,' he said, through the coughing that seemed to be usual with him these days. 'That Leanne.'

I snorted. He didn't know what he was talking about. I was the one who had perfected the art of juggling with seven flaming sticks while stark-bonking naked. And I knew I had made it perfectly clear to Mr Roberts that this was something Leanne had never quite managed to do correctly herself. She'd been too scared. What was so smart about that?

I was annoyed at how Mr Roberts always stuck up for Leanne. The other day he'd been cross with me for the hard time I gave her. He thought I should have been nicer considering the rough period she'd gone through when her father had run off, and her mother blamed Leanne before she took up with that conman posing as an aristocrat and didn't want Leanne living at home any more.

'Would you believe that much bad luck?' he coughed.

I shrugged. You make your own luck.

So perhaps it was jealousy that persuaded me one day to get rid of Leanne just like that. Whatever the reason, it was surprisingly easy.

She'd come from nowhere and one day, I told Mr Roberts, she went back to that place. I came to school and there was another girl sitting in Leanne's chair. A not so nice girl. A big spotty one, I told Mr Roberts peeking down the ladder at him so I could enjoy his look of disappointment. This girl had greasy pigtails, blackheads all over her nose and a cross-eyed look about her. I'd gone to Madame Gilligan to find out what had happened but all she said was that Leanne wasn't coming back any more. I went round to her house that afternoon and when I rang the bell, a scruffy looking woman with two snotty kids hanging onto her skirt answered the door. No forwarding address had been left.

No more questions asked. No answers given. People vanish into thin air every day and no one misses them.

NINETEEN

You see, Miranda was wrong.

People *can* come from (and go to) nowhere. The homeless Molly Mr Roberts took home with him from the Church café to his stationery shop was a monster he had created himself with every question he had asked during that first cup of tea we'd had together.

And that Molly was now a shared production. What with Miranda looking after my exterior appearance and Liz taking care of the inside thoughts, it felt a bit as if I had only a small part in the play.

It was only in the park with Tim that I had to think about being the real Molly. After I'd told him about Jessica, I carried on telling him the truth. I told him about Mr Roberts, and how I actually liked how I could make up things to tell him. I said how I didn't really like the hairstyles Miranda gave me, but I liked the attention she gave me. How the books Liz picked out for me told me more about her than she realised. I admitted to Tim how I missed having a television to watch but how I'd lie in bed some-times and imagine I was one of the girls from the pictures I had on the wall and all the wonderful things I'd be doing if I were her.

What I didn't tell him about was how I did this so I'd stop looking at my mother's picture. I punished myself at night some-times because I knew that, without me, she wouldn't take the second chance at life I wished for her. Instead she'd go back to my father. She'd said no to him only once before when she took me away, but she wasn't strong enough to do it again. So even as I told myself I was opening up my heart to Tim, I knew that the truths I was telling him about were only those about what was happening now. Never then.

It didn't seem to matter. Tim lived almost entirely in the present. He never wanted to know about the past, or the future. I'd never been with anyone like that before. When I told Tim anything, he didn't absorb it as just another story that didn't need acknowledgement, like Liz, or turn away from it, like Miranda. He listened to what it was I was really saying, even when it was hidden under layers of other words. He was more like the counsellor at school but better, because it wasn't his job. He wasn't being paid to listen to me. Although the counsellor pretended to be really interested in me, I could imagine that she'd forget about me the minute I shut the door to her office. I'd be like Leanne to her. Someone you could get rid of when they weren't convenient any more. A blank line in the register after I didn't show up a few times.

TWENTY

I'd gone through all the books on Liz's list so I was hoping she'd recommend some more the next time I went to the library, but I could see her over by the cookery section pulling out books for a frazzled young man who kept running his hands through his hair until it stuck up like a hedgehog. I smiled in anticipation of the story I knew she'd tell me about him later, and walked over to fiction to look for something on my own.

First, I tried running my finger over the books but none jumped out at me, so I looked for titles that sounded interesting. For some reason today, they all seemed the same. I was about to give up and wait until Liz was free when I saw a black spine. *The Story of O.*

I pulled the book out and without looking inside, took it to the desk.

Liz was stamping three cookery books out as the young man drummed his fingers on the counter.

'She'll love it,' Liz said. 'Remember to use proper chocolate.'

He grunted at her before thrusting the books into his rucksack.

She raised her eyebrows at me when he'd gone. 'First meal he's cooked for a woman,' she said. 'He'd better get the food right because he's not exactly a sparkling conversationalist.'

As I waited for her to go on, she picked up the book I'd chosen. 'Are you sure?' she asked, turning it over.

Suddenly I wasn't, but I didn't like it when Liz acted as if no one could do anything sensible without her. I nodded firmly.

'I suppose it's all right,' she said. 'And maybe you're ready for it, the way you've been gobbling up the others. Besides it's French, just how you like, although it's a bit more interesting than some of them.'

It was only when I'd got outside the library that I looked at the book properly.

There were none of the usual clues about the author in the inside pages. This was disappointing. I liked to keep that photograph of the writer in my mind. Never mind. I flicked through the pages as I walked, read first one paragraph and then another. Quickly I shut the book, hot cheeked, worried that some one might see me reading something like this. I imagined my father coming towards me, his arm held up about to hit me.

A line of schoolgirls wearing brightly checked dresses and straw hats walked straight by me. Had the teacher noticed my book? Two women in identical black leather jackets strolled by hand-in-hand. Had they seen? The old man with the walking stick? The frizzy-haired mother pushing a pram? Could they have read the cover?

There was no way I was going to be able to sleep that night. I sat up with the book, holding it in one hand, my other covering my mouth. The descriptions were vivid, too vivid. This was a world too far. It was like the prostitutes in Amsterdam all over again. I thrust it under the bed where I couldn't see it, but even that was too close. Eventually I put the book outside on the window ledge. I didn't even care if it rained. Let it get wet.

I went straight back to the library to find Liz the next morning. She was down on her hands and knees, clearing out the 'T' section. I knelt down next to her.

'Bugger the Trollopes,' she said. 'Both of them. They get every-where.'

She put one knee up, rubbing it where the ribbed thread of the carpet had left tracks on her skin.

'What was that all about?' I asked her, taking the book from the carrier bag I'd wrapped it up in and pushing it across the floor with the edge of my hand so I didn't have to touch it too much. 'It's horrible. I hated it. There was nothing good in it. Nothing good at all. It made me feel dirty.'

Liz took the book from me. 'Come with me,' she said. We went outside into the courtyard garden. It was a hot day, the lightest May wind was blowing, the sun was warm to the skin. We sat on the wooden chairs. I couldn't look at her.

'*The Story of O* is one of the finest love stories ever written by a woman to a man,' she said quietly, batting away a bee. 'You said you wanted to know everything about love.'

'I don't believe that book was written by a woman! No woman would want to be treated like that. It's unnatural,' I said. 'The things they make her do. She must be mad to write that book, to think of all those things. She wants putting away. And it's not love. Don't say that. Not even my father . . .' I stopped myself just in time.

'It was written by a sophisticated woman who was worried that her lover was going to get bored with her,' Liz continued as if I hadn't spoken. 'The book was written in sections, each one sent to the man as an example of how much, and in what depth, a woman is prepared to humiliate herself for the love of a man.'

'But why would she do that?' The smell of honeysuckle and summer jasmine in the library garden made me homesick for Colette's world. There, when the men got bored with them, the women retired into a land of summer gardens where they held tea parties full of arching roses, gossip and bridge with other old women. They took pleasure in the small things of life, like the strands of expensive pearls they'd once been given, a letter sent from an old flame, a sensational piece of someone else's bad luck. They didn't let masked men lead them around like dogs on a chain. Or worse. Much, much worse. I didn't want to have to think about it. I hated Liz at that moment.

'Why does anyone do anything?' Liz shrugged her shoulders. 'It worked though. The book kept the man's attention on the author. She won.'

Despite my disgust, I couldn't let it go just yet. 'But she didn't win though, did she?' I spoke more decisively than I meant to. 'The man was interested in O, the character, not the writer. So she lost him doubly. He only wanted her for something she'd made up. She was nothing herself. It's sick.' As I spoke I could feel my cheeks redden, tears coming to my eyes. I was aware of Liz looking at me sharply.

'You didn't find it arousing at all?' she asked. She spoke as plainly as if she was asking one of her other customers whether they were aware that their books were a day overdue.

'No!'

'Some women do,' she said. And then, after a pause during which I kept silent to show just how sick I thought it all was, she continued: 'It can be empowering to give up your life for someone else's pleasure like O did.'

I thought about this. From what I had read, O didn't give up anything. She seemed too actively passive for that, but it was hard to explain this to Liz. 'It can't have been worth it,' I said flatly. 'She was nothing in the end. Just an O. A big fat zero.'

'Maybe that's what we all are. In the end,' Liz said, but she was gentle in the way she spoke and she rested her hand on my arm. It was the first time she'd touched me. It reminded me of Mum and how when things had got really bad, all I wanted was for her to give me a hug and for us to laugh together. Maybe if we had managed to do that towards the end, even just the once, I wouldn't have had to leave.

'I'm not,' I said. 'I'm not nothing.'

Liz burst out into a peal of giggles. It definitely was one of the things I liked best about her, that healthy gust of happiness that couldn't help but make you smile back at her, marvelling at such a hidden, unexpected side to her. I couldn't stay angry with her any longer.

'Do you know what?' she asked. 'I don't know quite what you are, Little Miss Molly, but you're right about one thing. I don't think you'll ever be nothing. So go on with you. Tell me more about your young man. Bet you don't need to write him a book in order to get him to do what you want.'

TWENTY-ONE

'You want me to get you the bear?' Tim asked.

'The bear,' I nodded.

'I can't.' Tim was sitting on the top of the bench, leaning over as far as he could, his feet hooked under the seat to keep him anchored. 'It's not mine to give.'

'But it's in a shop so it's going to be someone's one day,' I pointed out. 'Why shouldn't it be mine? It would be like rescuing it. It'll bake in that hot shop and we need something cool to take our minds off this weather.' I flapped my skirt out in front of me so air could reach my legs. Mr Roberts's newspaper had been full of stories about the sudden record-breaking sunny weather although I noticed how he was carrying on wearing a vest under his shirt and a carefully knotted tie for the shop. Mind you, he was coughing even harder if possible and complaining of a cold that wouldn't go away.

'We could go and visit it, I suppose.' Tim came up straight again and beamed at me. His hair was tousled and thick at the front. I sat on my hands to stop myself brushing it straight. There was something so childish about him at times. 'Would you like that? You're always saying about us going places.'

'No. Not just to look. I want to have the bear otherwise there's no point.'

'What about going to listen to the happy woman then?' Tim was gently pushing my hands away now that I'd let them go. Just as I thought, they'd flown straight up to his hair and were trying to tidy it. 'She's bound to be on the phone again.'

'She's miserable really,' I said. 'She came into the shop one day and you could tell.'

'Really?' Tim bounced on to the bench so he was squatting next to me. I rested my elbows on his knees, and smiled up at him. 'Hello you,' he said, kissing me.

'Hello.' I tried to catch his mouth for more, running my tongue over his crooked teeth, but he moved away.

'So how could you tell she was unhappy exactly?'

I thought back to when she'd come in. I'd hidden behind the counter at first, scared she'd recognise me until I realised that although I'd been watching her, she had no idea who I was. It was a strange, powerful feeling. 'She had this walk,' I said. 'A sort of heel-sole walk. Happy people always prance on tiptoes.'

'Show me.'

I laughed but stood up, walking – no, prancing – up and down the path in front of Tim. He was sitting back on the bench watching me like the perfect audience I used to dream of when I was younger and would have given anything to play games like this.

'Now do unhappy,' he demanded.

I sloped along, shoulders hunched, heels slapping down aimlessly on the path behind me. Heel-sole.

'Jealous.'

I stopped and thought about this, and then put my shoulders right back, my chest forward and stared right ahead at him, my whole heart open for anybody to mock.

'Scared.'

I scampered, my foot hitting the ground lightly, my body as small as I could make it. But then, without warning, the feeling took over and I could almost hear the blood start to race through my body, my hands flapping at my sides as if I wanted to hit out at somebody, although it was me I was hurting. The bones in my head were tightening so they pressed against my brain.

'That's good,' Tim clapped. 'We can really do something with this. It'll be useful for the project. And now . . .'

I sat back on the bench and blew air out through my lips. I wanted to empty myself of all of that had gone before. 'Tim,' I said, 'just kiss me.'

Later, I sat in the changing room at the leisure centre and watched the television. It was on mute but I could work out what was going on from the scrolling headlines that ran along the bottom.

On the screen, a middle-aged man was wiping sweat off his brow with a white cotton handkerchief, as behind him, a woman looked on blank-eyed. The reporter leaned forward in front of them, talking urgently into the camera.

Sudden heat wave tragedy, I read. *Schools send children home.*

There was film of a group of children splashing in a river which reached only up to their knees. They were laughing as they poured water over each other and themselves. One boy lifted up his arms and the camera caught the glistening drops which poured through his fingers. He did it again and again, laughing as he eventually put his mouth down to drink from his cupped hands.

Doctors warn about disease threat, the caption read.

I hurried back to my room and made notes. For once, I ignored the two packets of Smarties and the doughnut I'd bought for my supper. I had an idea.

The next morning, despite the three fans Mr Roberts had put on at full-blast, the shop was still hot and airless. I stood up at the top of the ladder and let a trickle of sweat run down my upper lip before catching it with my tongue. My head was resting on my arms and I lifted my hair up to let any breeze around blow on to my neck. If I leant my nose into my skin, I could smell the musky scent of animal sweat.

'There was this guy who liked to take me to bathrooms,' I said. 'Not the one in his house, or anything. He'd book into a hotel, and ring me with the room number. I couldn't go straight up though. He preferred me to wait in the lobby. I'd sit on one of those little chairs they leave out, flicking through the newspapers or the hotel brochures until he came.

'He'd always say the same thing when he walked up to me. He'd pretend he was part of the hotel staff, that they'd had a complaint about how dirty I was, and he was wondering what could be done about it.

'I had to look ashamed then. If I was feeling really in the mood, I'd even pretend to cry.

'I'd tell him that I had nowhere to wash. I'd beg him to take pity on me and he'd ask me then about the conditions I lived in. That's what seemed to excite him as much as anything. I told him how I lived in a room with no bathroom, no proper washing facilities.'

I looked down at Mr Roberts as I said this, but all I could see was the kidney-shaped bald patch on top of his head. I guessed he was getting the message though. I was spending precious time going to the leisure centre for showers every evening in this hot weather. Time I could be spending with Tim.

'He asked me if I wasn't worried about getting diseases, even fleas. "Look at your hair," he'd say, lifting up a lock of my hair and letting it fall in disgust, although, of course,' I added, 'my hair was always perfectly clean.'

Mr Roberts gave a sort of snort from below. He was always teasing me about how many times Miranda did my hair.

I continued. 'He'd say then that he had to see what he could do about it. He hummed and hawed and looked at me over these big glasses he used to wear. And then he'd send me upstairs in the lift. I had to go and stand outside the hotel room and wait for him. He would always have these big bags with him. I was worried the first time, but they were just full of towels. He'd bring his own.

'We'd go straight to the bathroom. Candles were placed everywhere which he would light but the bath would already be full of water. Cold water, as clear and sparkling as if it was ice. I'd have to fold my clothes up as I took them off. He requested that especially, he wanted everything to be neat. And he wouldn't touch me, wouldn't even look at me directly as I did so. Just watched my reflection in the mirror. And when I was naked, he'd turn round and point towards the bath. He'd be fully dressed, although when I was in the bath, he'd put on one of those blue and white striped butcher's aprons. He'd kneel down beside me, take out a big white sponge from his bag and start to clean me. Not with soap or anything, just with the water.

'It was freezing sometimes. I'd catch my breath when he trickled it over me, but I never complained. Never said anything. Neither of us did. He'd rub me all over, pushing me back gently to immerse my hair in the water, spending time stroking my breasts with the sponge, dipping in between my legs and then back again to my breasts. He'd let water trickle down my back, following the curve of my spine. And then when he'd done it all, he'd do it again. We were there for hours.

'When he'd had enough, he'd get up and stand again with his back towards me, looking in the mirror. I used to fall into a kind of trance so I'd have to wake myself up sometimes. I'd wrap myself up in one of the white towels he'd brought and he'd come and rub me dry. And then I'd get dressed and leave.'

'That was that?'

'That was all,' I said. 'He never touched my skin directly once. He always used the sponge. He was a perfect gentleman.'

Mr Roberts was quick to step out of the way as I came down

the ladder. And when he came back from his lunchtime walk, I noticed a carrier bag by the door up to my room. 'What's this?' I asked.

'A present,' he said, bustling round with the till so he didn't have to take too much notice of me. 'Thought it might come in useful upstairs in this hot weather.'

Later that night, I filled the large bucket Mr Roberts had given me with cold water from the downstairs sink and carried it up to my room. Then I lit the candle he'd bought and using the white sponge I'd also found in the bag, I trickled cold water all over my naked body. It was like being baptised. I didn't rub myself dry with the matching towel though. Instead, I draped it out over the floorboards and lay down, letting the air from the open window dry my skin naturally. I emptied my mind of everything, breathing in and out slowly as I imagined myself a glass bear sitting on an ice cap watching the ocean swell before me.

TWENTY-TWO

Even when there was no chance of seeing Tim, I looked forward to my daily visits to the Seize the Day bench. I felt smug, sitting on Jessica's bench, safe in the bubble of my new worldly wisdom, confident that I'd found that other way out of an uncertain future that she had been searching for.

I went to the park one Thursday morning to find the bin had been moved, just how I wanted it. The concrete patch it had stood on still remained, but they'd cut the grass carefully around it.

'It's much better, isn't it?' I told Jessica. 'I think I know who arranged this. Tim. But we won't say anything. Not if he doesn't want us to. We'll get more flowers, surround you with beautiful things.' I was thinking of asking Tim to build an arch over the bench so I could grow honeysuckle through it, extending the bed all round the outside and planting spring bulbs for next year, bringing in pots of lilies to hide the rough concrete.

Afterwards I was walking back to the stationery shop, pausing across the road from the salon so I could wave at Miranda, when a hand touched my arm. I jumped.

'Molly! Molly Drayton, isn't it?' I turned round to see a small guy in a basketball top standing in front of me looking pleased with himself. 'I thought it was you. Haven't seen you since school. It's me. Joe.'

'Joe,' I repeated dully. He'd been an occasional member of one of the gangs of boys who used to stand outside my door and anger my father so. 'What are you doing here?'

'This is a coincidence,' he said. 'I'm only here because my orthodontist is stuck out in the back of beyond. I suppose the rents are cheaper.' He checked himself then, rubbed his finger over his perfectly straight teeth. 'Don't tell me you live here now?'

I nodded, and he looked embarrassed for about a second before continuing. 'Anyway, what are you doing back in town? I thought you'd gone to London with your mother. I hadn't heard you'd seen anyone from school. I don't blame you, mind. St Mary's is such a dump, although I will admit it was different in sixth form. I ended up being head boy for my sins.'

'That must have been nice,' I said.

'I've just been trekking through Asia for the last month. It was wild, you know.' I looked at the coloured bracelets on his tanned arms and nodded as if I did know. 'All being well, I've got a place at Oxford for October anyway,' he said. 'Reading English.'

'That's nice,' I repeated.

'And what about you? Any ideas? Art was always your subject, wasn't it?'

'It was nice,' I said. I'd turned into a goldfish, opening and shutting my mouth with nothing of any substance coming out. It wasn't that I couldn't think what to say, it was just that I couldn't slot back into being the particular Molly Drayton he thought I was. 'Anyway, I must go. Things to do and all that, you know.'

'You can't just go like that. It's been ages. Don't you want to know how everybody is?'

'Of course,' I lied.

'Go on. Ask me any name and I'll tell you what they're doing. I keep up with everyone. It's kind of my thing.'

I stared at him. 'Leanne,' I said.

He paused. 'Can't remember her,' he said eventually. 'Was she in your year, or mine?'

'Mine,' I said. 'Anyway, I did hear something about how she's gone to France. I think she's in show business or something. It sounded very exciting anyway.'

He laughed, the kind of condescending laugh I suddenly remembered the kids at school always used when they felt they'd been caught out. 'Leanne. I think I'm remembering something now. And you? What are you up to?'

I imagined him in the pub later, with all the others. Sitting round the table, talking and laughing, just how I'd used to envy them. 'Guess who I bumped into today,' he'd say. 'Molly Drayton. You remember that stunner from year ten. She's gone off a bit now, mind you. Got fat.' And then they'd all start remembering, although him best of all because knowing other people's business was 'his thing'. 'Wasn't there something odd about her?' he'd say. 'Something about her father.' They'd huddle together, just as they used to when I watched them. Before I had to rush off to make sure my father didn't catch me, because even looking would have got me into trouble.

I swallowed the fear down. I needed to keep in control. 'This and that,' I said. 'I'm in retail now, working my way up to the top, you know.'

'Good for you. I'd prefer to do something practical too, but my parents are kind of fixed on me going to Uni. Hey, maybe we could have a coffee or something when I've finished at the dentist?'

'That would be nice,' I said. 'I can't today but I'll give you a ring.' At last I turned to leave.

'Wait. You don't have my number.' He was scrabbling in his pocket for a piece of paper or something.

'No, really,' I said. 'I've got to go.'

He shrugged. 'Well, maybe I'll catch up with you another time,' he said.

'You too,' I said, stupidly. 'But I must get on. Time presses, you know.' I pushed past him, only half-looking over at the salon, although I could see Miranda standing at the window watching us intently.

'Molly.'

I stopped, although I didn't turn round. I was so frightened he was going to say he'd just remembered what the funny thing with my father was.

'I wish you well,' he said. And that was all, but I knew he meant it. For some strange reason, I wanted to cry. I ran into the shop.

Time presses. Pressed time. Did I really think I had the power to make time stand still? Was that even what I wanted any more?

TWENTY-THREE

The square mirror in the shop toilet was so small that when I leant forward to have a look at my teeth, the rest of me faded away until I became one huge mouth. I drew my lips right back and turned my head from side to side.

I'd finally got rid of my braces about two years ago, but seeing Joe had reminded me how you were supposed to keep going back regularly. My whole childhood used to be full of continual examinations and check-ups just to keep standing. They didn't seem to be necessary any more. Did that mean they never really were?

'Molly?'

I spooked my reflection with a brief imaginary roar before going back through to the shop to see what Mr Roberts wanted.

'Here she is. Now, Molly, there's someone I want you to meet.'

Mr Roberts was speaking in that phoney too-cheerful voice people always use for dogs, babies and wheelchair users. I was just looking round for the awkward customer, when I noticed the small pointy nosed woman by his side.

'This is my wife, Mrs Roberts,' he said. 'Here she is then, Joan. This is Molly.'

Mrs Roberts nodded at me.

'I hadn't told her about you before, see,' Mr Roberts said. He looked sheepish so I tried to smile in a non-threatening way at

Mrs Roberts. 'It must have completely slipped my mind, but as soon as I did, she insisted on rushing over here. She's good like that. She cares.'

Mrs Roberts gave me a stern once-over. I stopped smiling.

'Pleased to meet you,' I said, resisting the ridiculous urge to curtsey.

'And you too, I'm sure,' she said, and that's when I got a second surprise. Her accent was foreign, her voice husky. 'You aren't what I was expecting.'

'I think she'd got it into her head that you were some blonde bombshell,' Mr Roberts said. 'I told her don't be silly. She's just Molly. Molly's not like other girls. She doesn't care for all that stuff. Didn't I tell you that, Joanie? Well, are you satisfied?'

Mrs Roberts was looking round the shop now. 'And you sleep upstairs?' she asked.

I nodded. 'Would you like to see it?' I asked.

'Don't be silly, Molly,' Mr Roberts said quickly. 'Mrs Roberts doesn't want to be bothered with your room.'

Mrs Roberts stared at him, and he shut up. She turned back to me. 'Your parents know where you are?' she asked.

'Oh yes,' I said. I took a quick look at Mr Roberts but he was wheeling one of the office chairs across for Mrs Roberts to sit down on. She ignored it.

'I don't mind telling you it's lovely to see you here, pet. I know the shop isn't your thing,' he told her. 'We miss a woman's touch, what with it just being me and Molly.' He kept darting little glances at me as if he was daring me to say something stupid like I was a woman too, but Mrs Roberts was walking round the shop properly now, trailing her fingers over the shelves. She stopped once to look at the display of coloured pens I'd made one Thursday afternoon when no one had come into the shop. I'd pasted plain paper up on the wall, started drawing a garden of flowers which customers had added to as they tried out the different pens. I would take little kids there when they got bored of browsing with their parents. There were butterflies, trees, and one of the art students who came in had even drawn a little swing with a small blonde girl on it. We were running out of space.

Mr Roberts and I watched her in silence. He jerked his arm up once, when she rested her hands on the ladder, but other than that he seemed rooted to the spot. I was surprised to feel nothing. Just interest. I couldn't take my eyes off her. Mrs Roberts shook the ladder slightly, looked up at the shelves and then went back to her slow pacing around.

'Is this all your doing, Molly?' she asked, when she came back to us. 'The cleaning, sorting out the stock and making everything look so much nicer.'

I nodded.

'And you enjoy it?'

I nodded again, this time with real enthusiasm. 'I love—' I began but she interrupted me.

'And you are happy with your room?' she asked.

'It's just until I can get somewhere of my own,' I said. It was the first time I'd thought about moving from the shop, but it seemed to be the answer she'd been looking for.

'Then I think you are managing well without me,' she said. 'It all looks very satisfying compared to how it used to be with just my husband who really doesn't know how to make things nice. Very satisfying indeed. Jules, I have finished here. I will expect you back for dinner.'

He rushed over to open the door for her and as she was leaving the shop, I saw him take her elbow. I thought he was going to help her out, but he raised her hand to his lips and pressed his mouth against it. She looked over to where I was standing as if she'd known I was watching her all the time and she smiled very briefly at me, and then she was on her way. I raised my hand up in a kind of farewell salute.

Mr Roberts was beaming when he came back. He tried to bustle round, acting as if he was busy, but he couldn't keep it up.

'My wife is a remarkable woman,' he said. 'She keeps me well under control. I should have told her about you straight away. Although I don't mind telling you it gave me a bit of a shock when she insisted on coming round to meet you.'

'Is she French?' I asked.

'We've been married thirty years next September,' he said, ignoring me. 'The best decision I ever made.'

'They do say French women keep their looks when they get old,' I said.

'Old?' Mr Roberts looked cross. 'She's much younger than me.'

'Well . . .' I wanted to say something light-hearted about how that wasn't hard, but I didn't want to shatter this unexpectedly light mood. Apart from exchanging the 'information' Mr Roberts and I didn't usually speak much.

'I suppose I was comparing her to me,' I said.

He calmed down. 'Oh Molly,' he said. 'Everyone's old compared to you. You are a goose, but you've done well today. You must feel proud at how pleased Mrs Roberts was with your work. She doesn't give out compliments to just anyone.'

It was only later I noticed he'd folded the ladder up and put it away. He saw me looking at the shelf. 'Just tidying things up,' he said, turning too slowly for me not to see his blush.

TWENTY-FOUR

'So are you going to tell me about him?' Miranda asked when we met up for our afternoon ciggies later. 'Is he the great mystery of your life?'

It really was turning into the kind of hot summer you don't imagine ever coming to an end. The French restaurant had put tables out in the street, music blared from open car windows, people wore less clothes than they would on the beach and no one gave it a second thought. A mother and child walked past us now, both licking ice creams, drops dribbling down off the kid's chin.

'Him? That was Mrs Roberts,' I said. 'His wife. Ju-elle-ses wife.' The letters rolled round my mouth when I tried to copy her accent. I chased after them with my tongue. 'She's called Joo-ann.' It couldn't have been her proper name, surely. It didn't sound very French. It was difficult to roll that one anywhere.

'Jules? What are talking about? I meant that little chappie you were chatting up in the street.'

I had to think hard. Mrs Roberts's visit had wiped everything else from my mind and then I laughed. She meant Joe. 'Nope, that's only a boy I was at school with.'

'His hair could do with a good wash and condition.'

I hadn't noticed. 'So guess what – Mrs Roberts is French,' I said.

'Everybody knows that.'

I was shocked. 'I didn't,' I said. 'You could have told me.'

'What's it to do with anything? She never talks to anyone round here anyway. Typical Froggie, thinks she's much better than any of us. She even gets her hair done in London.'

'Froggie? You love France, Miranda. Brigitte Bardot, St Tropez and all that.'

'I used to.' Miranda tossed her head. 'You move on.'

She'd just had her highlights done by one of the other trainees, and although I'd told Miranda how super she looked, like a blonde Julia Roberts, it actually resembled more a mangy old lion at a cut-price zoo. It made me think even more of Mrs Roberts, having the good taste not to take risks like that.

'She said I made the shop look nice,' I told Miranda.

'And so you do, lovely. How many times have I said you're being exploited? You've a talent, you have. You should be on the telly doing that *Changing Rooms* programme. I bet you'd be better than any of them. You're prettier too.'

I couldn't help laughing. 'They're proper designers,' I said. 'They've had training and everything. You can't just get on television like that.'

'So go to college and train. There was this film we were watching at home last week about women in a university in America. Oh, the main woman, the teacher they all wanted to be like, she had lovely hair.' Miranda put her hand up to her head automatically and then glared at me. 'Or are you going to spend the rest of your life working in a stationery shop?'

'You're happy staying in the salon,' I pointed out. I wasn't sure what had brought on this attack.

'But that's different. Even if I do stay, I've a ladder I can progress up. I'm an assistant stylist now, soon I'll be a senior stylist and then I could even get my own chair. Anyway, I'm thinking of going back to college at nights. Study for some exams. Maybe I'll go to university or something. I love books and stuff, or I used to anyway.'

I stared at her. Ambition was never something I'd associated with Miranda before. 'I've got a ladder,' I laughed, suddenly thinking of Mr Roberts at the bottom with me at the top, but of course Miranda had no idea what I was talking about. 'For sorting out stock,' I added unnecessarily.

She shook her head as if I'd said something stupid again. This was becoming a habit with her. 'Anyway, what I wanted to say was that we were wondering if you were able to come and have tea with us one day.'

'We?'

'Mum, Dad and me.' Then she caught me smiling at her. 'Ooooh, you wicked minx. Just because you're falling over yourself with nice young men doesn't mean we all are.'

'Plato used to say that when the first man was created, he was too strong so God cut him in half,' I told her. Liz had been talking about this in the library. 'That's why we're always searching for our other side. When we fall in love, we complete everything we've been missing even though we haven't been aware of the gap.'

'If you say so,' Miranda sniffed. 'I might dream about silly things, but in real life I'll settle for someone nice-looking, decent and hard working. You can keep your Plato.'

'My Plato in the park,' I said.

'Sometimes you don't talk sense.'

I couldn't tell her because it would probably scare her and she'd never speak to me again, but if I loved anyone just at that very moment, it was Miranda. Every bit of her, from her silly hairstyle, to the handbag she carried that was so small she had to keep her cigarettes in her pocket, to her wobbly shoes and those big hoop earrings she always wore. I even loved her too low T-shirt with the lacing which stretched right across her enormous chest. Loving Tim made it so much easier to love other people.

'Your hair,' I said instead, 'I've been thinking about it. It's not really Julia Roberts at all.' She looked worried. 'No,' I continued, 'it's Jennifer Aniston but prettier. It's perfect.'

'Oh you,' she cooed before she wobbled back across the road, but I could tell she was pleased.

'Ve-rrry satisfying in-deeed,' I copied Mrs Roberts's voice as closely as I could remember as I walked back to the stationery shop, taking a final theatrical puff of my cigarette and grinding it out under the sole of my imaginary black stiletto shoe. Bugger being pretty, maybe if I'd just been born French then everything would have been all right.

TWENTY-FIVE

That night, I was sitting on the Seize the Day bench staring at a thin red ribbon that was tied to the young tree opposite. At first I thought it might have been put there by some kid mucking around, but I couldn't see any others in the park. It worried me in a way I couldn't describe.

'Hello.'

Tim was standing in front of me. I hadn't noticed him coming, but I was so happy to see him I burst out laughing. He'd told me he might have to go away again. 'I didn't expect you,' I said.

'But you're here, waiting for me. You must have sensed something.'

'Let me look at you,' I said. 'I've missed you.'

If you had to pick one thing to say about Tim's appearance, it would be that he was thin. His bones almost caved in on themselves with no flesh in between to hold them up. T-shirts flapped on him, trousers looked half-empty. When he held his arms up, the gaps around his body were more noticeable than the filled-in bits. His face was beautiful though. His cheekbones cut across like knives, his eyes were sunken under his thick eyebrows but were the bluest of blues so once you noticed them they seemed to be shining just for you, and his teeth were the straightest I'd ever seen. Under his chin, his Adam's apple bounced up and down even when he wasn't talking. But that wasn't the only thing about Tim's face that was mobile, his expression could flit from laughter to anger to passion within seconds, and back again. I could stare at Tim for hours.

Now, he sat there impassively as if he was a statue. His gaze was fixed on the path. He was wearing faded jeans and a navy T-shirt with the words 'No Angel' in yellow. I bent down and lifted up the hem of his jeans. Again no socks. I ran my finger over his ankle. His legs were surprisingly hairy.

A sudden jolt of desire for him took me by surprise. My hands were shaking so I placed them on my thighs to steady them, and myself. When I was finally able to look up, Tim had his eyes shut.

'Did your meeting go well?' I asked brightly. I wanted to get things back to normal.

'Meeting?' He opened one eye and raised his brow.

'Isn't that where you've been?' I said. 'You said you were going to advise someone, so I presumed you'd be meeting them.'

He nodded, both eyes were open now. He had his head on one side and was staring at me.

'So you were waiting for me?'

My heart turned over. I still had a residue of panic from my own feelings left inside but there was something else there too now. Filling me up so it was hard to breathe.

Fear?

Not really.

More a shiver of anticipation.

I let him pull me towards him, and waited for him to give me one of his kisses. His delicious kisses.

Instead he held on to the back of my head with both hands, his fingers splayed through my hair, nails scraping my scalp. I tried to rest back into him comfortably, relaxing my neck as if I wasn't scared. In biology once, we'd measured our heads, resting them on bathroom scales to check the teacher's statement that your head is a third of your body weight. As a scientific experiment it had been a disaster, but maybe that wasn't the point. I would have bet anything that the heaviness of our heads was one of the few things we'd learnt at school that none of us forgot.

I was half wondering now whether you put on weight in your head too when the rest of your body got fat and if so where would it go, when suddenly Tim yanked his hands tight against my scalp.

'Oy!' I tried to pull away but his fingers were entwined in my hair now and he wasn't letting go.

'Ow! Gerrof, Tim. That's sore.'

'So tell me again exactly how you knew I was going to be here.'

'I didn't.' I had to keep my head face down to stop him hurting me any more. 'I was coming to the bench anyway to speak to Jessica.'

'But you didn't know her. You told me that.'

'She's become like a friend now.'

'Jessica's dead. Are you telling me you have dead friends?'

I mumbled something I didn't quite understand myself. He relaxed his hold slightly but I didn't want to risk that pain again so I held my head still. I could taste that old familiar fear in my stomach, how I used to feel when my father got into one of his moods, the same sense that I had to think calmly, not to make things worse. I tried to concentrate on the individual strands of grass underneath the Seize the Day bench.

'I can't hear you,' Tim said, gently raising my face. He cupped my cheeks with both hands, looked deep into my eyes. 'What did you say?'

'I don't have any other friends but you,' I repeated. 'Only you.'

'Only me,' he said and then thankfully, at last, he smiled at me and with that same gentleness he moved his fingers over to trace my eyebrows, a fingertip skirting my nose. My lips parted as he rubbed them up and down and I darted my tongue out to lick his finger. But it was only after he bent his head down to kiss me that I relaxed. We walked back to my room hand in hand.

'Maybe we could go to your home one time?' I asked as we climbed up the back stairs of the stationery shop. Living in the present is all very well, but there were so many questions about Tim I didn't have the answer to. I didn't want to ask him direct because I was hiding secrets too.

'Nope, safer not to. There's no one looking out for me here,' he said, linking my fingers in his and stroking my hand with the pad of his index finger. We were in the room now, standing just the other side of the doorway. 'I have to be careful. I explained that.'

'Kiss it,' I said suddenly.

'What?'

'You know, lift my hand up to your mouth and kiss it. Like the French do.'

And without smiling, looking right at me, he let go of my hand straight away but then just when I was feeling like the biggest kind of idiot there was, he caught it again. He held my fingers very gently and pressed them against his lips, kissing each fingertip precisely.

I melted inside.

'Tell me something nice,' I said. It was that same 'wanting to eat him' feeling I'd had in the park. I was breathless with the possibility of power over him.

'You're beautiful,' he said. 'Inside and out.' But this time he sounded as if he was quoting something he could only vaguely remember.

Then I tried to pull him down next to me on the mattress, but he was too twitchy. He stood up and bounced up and down on the balls of his feet as if he was getting ready to run. He was breathing in and out deeply, as if he was measuring the air entering and exiting his body.

'Tim, sit down,' I said. 'You're making me nervous.'

'Can't we go back down and look round the shop?' he asked. 'There might be something useful for me to use in my work.'

'I suppose Mr Roberts wouldn't mind so long as we don't put the lights on. I've never done it before.'

I didn't know why I lied as I often walked round the shop in the dark at night, particularly when it was too hot to sleep. I liked to breathe in the smells. Sometimes, I even shut my eyes to experience them better – the dry wood whiff of paper; the petrol after-tang from the bottles of Tipp-Ex I opened; the strange sweetness of the glue sticks. I held paper files up to my face and tested to see if each different colour had an individual smell; opened notebooks at random to revel in the blankness of the empty pages. I even buried my whole face in the bowl of erasers, chewing into ones that caught accidentally in my mouth so I had to hide them afterwards in case puzzled customers complained to Mr Roberts of bite marks in their stationery goods.

'Come on. Let's explore.'

'Can't we just stay here?' Kiss my hand again, I was praying to him silently. And more. Let's play Colette and Cheri, but make it real. Let's climb Mr Roberts's ladder together and watch it rock. But I didn't say anything. I couldn't put my finger on why it was, but Tim seemed different tonight. All my courage was seeping out and there wasn't anything I could do about it.

'Are you frightened?' he asked.

I stared at him. He didn't seem to be mind-reading, he was smiling but not in the way he might if he knew what I'd been thinking. Just in case though I kept on talking to him in my head. I am scared, I told him silently, but I am more than six years old and I want more than your kisses. I want all the things I've been telling Mr Roberts about. But I want them to be sweet, not harsh and furtive. I want it all to be loving and gentle and sharing. Those things had to be real, I'd read about them in books. But Tim was right in one way. I wasn't brave any more. When I still didn't say anything out loud, he made for the door and I followed him quickly. I didn't want him wandering round the shop on his own.

And that's where it happened. Of all the places I used to imagine losing my virginity, the dusty floor of the stationery shop between the shelves of padded envelopes and the display of desk-top fans wasn't one of them. Although it probably wouldn't have come as any surprise to my father. Hadn't he always expected the worst of me?

As we walked round the shop in the dark, Tim had grabbed me unexpectedly, lifted up my skirt, prodded me painfully with his fingers. Then suggested we both lie on the floor, do it there. He asked if I wanted any money first. No, I said. No! I had a sudden picture of Mr Roberts taking notes from the till. It's all been taken care of then, Tim asked, and I said yes because I didn't know what he was talking about. Then he told me to take my pants off as he undid his trousers and got on top of me. I wondered if I should tell him it was my first time but it seemed rude to interrupt him. I just braced myself for the pain I'd read about. I was all set to be brave but . . . nothing. I could hardly even feel Tim come inside me, but he must have done because he humped up and down a few times on my stomach and then after a swift moan, rolled off. His back was turned towards me, his T-shirt pulled down now to hide his still bare bottom.

Was that it? I just lay there, looking up at the polystyrene squares on the ceiling. I felt numb. Not upset, or deliriously happy, or even slightly weepy. Just numb. Surreptitiously I put my hand down to feel between my legs. The skin on the inside of my thighs was wet. I didn't pinch. When I brought my fingers up again it was hard to see whether it was blood in the dark. I smelt my fingers, but they reeked of paper. The stationery shop at its driest and dustiest.

I shifted over to pull my pants up. I was worried Mr Roberts might be angry if I bled on his carpet.

Tim sat up too. He should hold me now, tell me I'd been a good girl, but he said nothing. I felt everything heave inside me, but I wasn't connected to my body. Not just at that moment. It had nothing to do with me any more.

'That was lovely,' I lied. 'Thank you.'

He nodded.

'So do you want to come upstairs?' I asked. 'There's room for us both to sleep on my mattress.'

'I'd better go,' he said.

'Please stay. We could do it again.' To my horror, I could feel tears prick at the back of my eyes. 'Please, Tim. I love you. Don't go. Perhaps we could go for a drink? To the pub?'

'Another time,' he said. 'I've really got to leave. You'll be fine, er...'

I had a sudden realisation that he couldn't remember my name.

'Molly,' I said, trying not to cry.

He turned his back to me as he pulled his trousers up and buckled his belt in a businesslike manner.

'Please don't go,' I begged again. 'Not like this.' I put out my hand to hold on to his jeans.

'Molly,' he said then, deliberately, looking down at me, nodding as if he finally recognised me. 'I'm so sorry, Molly. I'm not all right in myself. I'm sorry. I don't know what came over me then. I shouldn't have let that happen. Not to you. Can't you understand that?' He kept brushing his hair off his face. Again and again.

I felt ashamed of myself. But before I could tell him that it was all right and how I'd really wanted him to do everything he did, he left. He didn't wait for me to answer.

TWENTY-SIX

Three days.

That was all it took for Mr Roberts to put the ladder back up. I was helping a customer in the front with a special order and when I turned round quickly, I caught sight of him clicking the top rungs together.

Not now. I shut my eyes as my stomach lurched. Please not now. I looked over to the spot where Tim and I had made love. Nothing. Not even a stain. I moved over to the window so I could see the corner of Miranda's hair salon. It felt like a comfort blanket, knowing she'd be inside. The customer was drawing a flower on my poster with one of the new glitter pens now.

'Oh, look at this,' she said suddenly, her pen stopping in mid-air. I came to stand beside her.

Above the flowers, someone had drawn a male and a female angel, floating hand-in-hand in the sky. The male angel was thin and thick eyebrowed, his cartoon mouth a straight line turned down at the edges, but the female was smiling and round-bellied. Her blue eyes dominated her face and her long hair floated behind her. Both angels had been outlined with a gold sparkling pen and strands of glitter glue bled out to add to the effect. A polar bear stood in the background, standing on top of a mountain shining with silver ink, surrounded by a circle of silver and gold stars.

'It's lovely,' the customer laughed. 'Do you know the girl almost looks like you?'

113

I knew who had drawn it, but it was so detailed I wasn't sure how Tim had managed it without me noticing him. Had he come back? I put my finger out to touch it. 'Lovely,' I repeated. When she went back to colouring in her flower, I had to resist brushing her hand away. I didn't want anything to spoil Tim's message to me. He was looking after me. Everything was going to be OK.

The customer finally left, after putting back half of what she'd collected. 'I suppose you get a discount,' she said and I nodded although I'd never thought of this before. My life, as it stood, was totally devoid of any need for stationery, of any form of record at all. Maybe this was why I held on to her rejected pencil case, putting it under the counter until I decided what to do with it.

The poster I took off the wall and whisked upstairs to my room where it would be safe. I wanted to spend some time studying it closely to see if Tim had drawn anything else I'd missed.

Downstairs I sat behind the counter to wait for Mr Roberts to call me, and thought of Tim.

'It's quiet in here.' Mr Roberts came out of the kitchen, drying his hands. 'But never mind. Nice for the two of us to have some peace.'

'It's been very busy,' I lied. 'I expect there will be more customers soon.'

'Now, Molly.'

That was all he needed to say to make me realise procrastinating would be no use. Just those two words. *Now. Molly.*

Without thinking, my fingers walked over the keys of the cash register to spell out Mum's telephone number. When I realised what I was doing, I put them up to my mouth and started sucking on the tips to distract myself.

'I stole something precious from someone once,' I said

114

suddenly, watching Mr Roberts to see how long it would take him to sneak a quick look at the cash register.

'It was this thing I'd been begging for, but it wasn't ever going to be mine so I decided to take it by any means.'

Mr Roberts coughed into his handkerchief. 'It was from one of the teachers at school,' I said. I shut my eyes to remember the smell of the biology lab. The dust from the wooden floors, the chemical sweetness coming from the jars of glass bottles lined up on the shelves, the rancid water from a vase of flowers that had been used in an experiment and left too long. 'She'd just left her bag lying around one day and I took my chance to nick some money. I'd never done it before.'

'I've been thinking about the shelves at the back,' Mr Roberts said. 'The top ones. They could do with a bit of sorting out. Let's do it now, while the shop's clear.'

It wasn't a question. He was looking at me directly. Now. Molly. Now.

'I thought if I was caught I'd say I was hungry,' I continued, once I was on top of the ladder. 'Make them all feel sorry for me but I went straight out to buy some new clothes instead.' I was leaning against the shelf, resting my cheek on one of my hands, the other aimlessly shifting a box an inch this way and that. 'I got these red shoes, glittering with sequins and with a long black shiny ribbon on the heel which fluttered every time I took a step. I wore a little pleated black skirt and a red beret with it. And the brightest red lipstick you could imagine,' I added.

I liked myself in this outfit. I could imagine prancing down the High Street with everyone smiling at me. I kicked back my own shoe now, and narrowly avoided thumping Mr Roberts on the forehead.

'Careful!' he warned.

He must have been stretching his head up. I didn't want to think about what he might have been doing. Good job I'd got trousers on. I put my hand down, pulling the denim an inch away from my body. All my clothes seemed to be getting looser these days. I got back to the story quickly. Molly in red. I shut my eyes to imagine it better.

'I climbed on a bus in the middle of town,' I said. 'I didn't even look where it was going. I had some new clothes on my back, and some change left in my pocket. It was an adventure. To begin with I sat up by the driver but then I made myself move back a row every time the bus stopped. Whoever I sat next to, I had to do whatever they asked me to do. It was a rule I set myself.

'The first few times I sat next to women. The first one asked me to get her coat off the rack. That was easy. The next was about seventeen, not much older than me. She was a country girl, as plump as an apple just about to fall off the tree. And as spotty too. Not like the supermarket ones. She was all wrapped up in an old beige mackintosh. It was only when the bus jolted and I fell against her that I felt the roundness of her breasts.'

Mr Roberts gasped audibly below me. What had I just said? Breasts. Was that all it took to make him happy, for me to say breasts a few times?

'They were big breasts.' I paused. No second gasp. I carried on with my bus ride.

'I did it again a few times, every time the bus went round the corner, putting my cheek against her chest as if by accident even when I could see she was starting to get annoyed. She still didn't say anything though. Just gazed firmly out of the window.

'I wanted her to ask me to do something, just for fun, so I thought I'd start the ball rolling. I asked her if she was going far but she just turned round and stared at me. Then the bus stopped and she got off, but not before giving me such an unpleasant look.

'I lost interest after that and then someone came to sit next to me. I didn't look up at first and when I did, I saw it was a man. He was smiling at me in a nervous way which made me feel more in charge. I forgot about the breast woman and concentrated on this new possibility.

'I think I must be dreaming,' he said and I could tell that he meant I was the sort of woman he'd probably always dreamt of. And I suppose I was, in my red beret and high heels.

'I didn't speak, just opened my handbag, got out my lipstick and looking at my reflection in the window, I put another layer of red on. Then I smacked my lips together and smiled at him. In my mind, I could see the breast woman, her mackintosh clutched together over her chest with one hand, a sort of yearning expression on her face. I looked straight into the eyes of the man next to me. Or as straight as I could.

'He was older, you see. About as old as you.'

And then I stopped talking. I just shut my eyes and put my forehead down on the shelf. I wasn't sure I could handle this, not just at the moment.

'Older, eh?' Mr Roberts was egging me on, willing me to get back to the tale. He didn't seem to care how the story ended, but I knew he'd be hoping that I'd fall into some kind of trouble. That I'd be humiliated and hurt and somehow damaged. For those were the stories he seemed to prefer now that it was clear Leanne wasn't coming back.

I squeezed my eyes tightly together. If there were any tears there to fall, now was the moment. I was sure I could look down and call on Mr Roberts's sympathy. Remind him what a good job his wife thought I was doing, and then he'd tell me to climb down. Normal life resumed. I remained dry-eyed though. Resolute.

'Have you gone to sleep on me up there, Molly?' Mr Roberts gave the ladder a gentle shake. 'What did he ask you to do?'

I clutched at the edge of the shelf automatically. If you put a newborn baby above a washing line and drop them, they'll be able to hold on with their hands. Even from birth, the body is designed to hold its own weight. That was another fact I'd kept in my head from school.

'Still awake,' I said. 'I was just thinking about something.'

He coughed. 'I'm just going to get a glass of water,' he said. 'You stay right there.'

He didn't wait for an answer. I shoved the box this way and that, not angrily though. I was thinking. By the time he came back, I was ready.

'The trouble was that it was my stop,' I said. 'As I got off, I could see the older man standing up too. He was going to follow me but I shook my head. I wanted to be on my own.'

I stopped talking suddenly.

'Is that it?' Mr Roberts said. He sounded oddly subdued and wouldn't meet my gaze when I looked down at him, his eyes slipping away to the floor. His face was still flushed from coughing.

'I think so,' I said, coming down the ladder.

'It was different. Not up to how it used to be with Leanne.' Mr Roberts made way for me as I brushed past him. He put his hand out to touch my waist.

'I know,' I said, slipping away from his grasp. 'I'll tell you more tomorrow. If the shop's quiet. Although I'm a bit embarrassed about it because that man did follow me home after all and he asked me to do lots of things you can only imagine. It doesn't really show me in the best light.'

Mr Roberts smiled, his shoulders almost visibly bounced with relief. 'Now Molly,' he said. 'You haven't been a wicked girl again, have you?'

* * *

That night, the receptionist at the leisure centre waved me through to my shower without any need for queuing or paying.

The first time it had happened, I'd enjoyed this privilege but now there was something too pathetic about my little plastic bag filled with towel and soap for there to be anything but humiliation. Sometimes others in the queue waiting for their wholesome swim or half hour on the badminton court would look at me with a too frank interest.

That only made me hurry through quicker.

Once I was in the showers, I turned the water on hard to drown out everyone and everything else. Perhaps I should buy a swimming costume. For the moment though, I tried to put the outside world aside and concentrate on my shower.

I washed myself again and again, rubbing my skin hard with the flannel Mr Roberts had brought me. When all the soap was rinsed off, I turned the water to freezing. And then I stood there, grimacing as the sharp needles hit me. As I turned to ice.

TWENTY-SEVEN

The next day I went up to the Seize the Day bench to plant two pansies I got from the shop on the High Street. One red and one blue. I was going to put them on either side of the bench, but then I changed my mind and placed them next to each other, at a slight angle so it looked more artistic. I had to use a spoon to dig the hole so it took some time, but it was satisfying. Then I went to the water fountain and carefully carried some water over in my cupped hands to baptise them. Grow well, I whispered.

I buffed up Jessica's brass plaque with the edge of my T-shirt until it shone – *just like your hair used to*, I told her – and cleared up the dead leaves from round the base of the young tree that was growing in front of the bench.

Only when everything was shipshape, did I sit down. To begin with, I pretended not to see Tim zigzagging from tree to tree across to me. Not in a weird fashion but just so he was in sight for such a short time that you hardly noticed him.

'Herrrr-hummm,' he said when he reached the bench, looking up under his eyebrows and doing a waggly thing with his fingers as he pointed his hands towards me. Then he came and sat down without saying anything more. Just seeing him made me crinkle up with happiness.

You see there was something I'd felt when I was watching Tim come towards me. It was the way I caught myself looking at him. It wasn't so much that I thought 'oh there's Tim,' but that I absorbed my vision of him right into me, so I knew who he was before my eyes took in the boring exterior details. And then as he came closer, I could feel every muscle, every bone working away under his skin. I willed him to keep straight on, but the funny thing was that my thoughts were so much inside him at that stage I was convinced that if the fancy took me, I would be able to get him to veer off in a different direction. Or even skip or jump. Anything I wanted. And he wouldn't be able to do a thing about it.

And then when he sat down next to me and did that gasping thing of his, everything of mine that had been in him a minute ago slotted back into place between us so I felt a rush of peace. I didn't even have to touch him to feel us coming together.

We recognised each other, Tim and me. Not just boring names or who we were, but all we had been and all we could be too. That was when I knew nothing more was asked of us when we were together than just being; what we had was plenty enough. I was going to ask him what had really gone on that night in the shop, but it was too nice, both of us sitting there like that. 'I'm happy,' I told him.

'And so am I.' His fingers moved to hold on to mine, and I rested my head on his shoulder.

'Tim?'

'Herummmm,' he replied.

'Just that,' I said. 'Just Tim.'

It was quiet in the shop for the whole of the following day. Mr Roberts shut himself up in the kitchen with a hot cup of tea – Mrs Roberts's orders, he said, although I was sure the whisky he was lacing it with liberally wasn't her idea – and the shop was empty, so he said I could nip out for a break some time. I went to ask Miranda when she was free.

She was blow-drying an old lady's hair, but beckoned for me

to sit down and wait. I flicked through a magazine I'd read before until the expression on Miranda's customer caught my attention. She had her eyes wide open, a blissful smile on her powdered face as she watched Miranda gently twist the curlers out and brush her hair so it circled her head like a silver halo.

'They come alive like flowers,' Miranda told me, after she'd helped the woman on with her coat and taken her to the desk to pay. 'I love doing the old people best, you know. It means more.'

I tried to hold back the shudder. 'Her scalp was so pink,' I said. 'It was like you could see everything underneath. Disgusting.'

Miranda stared at me. 'I'm going to the library in my lunch hour,' she said. 'You can come too.'

At lunchtime she knocked on the stationery shop window and we walked up to the library together.

'This is nice,' I said. I was gushing because Miranda wasn't saying much. 'We should go out more. Have a drink in the pub and stuff.' If Tim wouldn't come with me, maybe Miranda would.

'Maybe.' But Miranda seemed doubtful as she pushed the heavy library doors open. It was almost a relief when Liz came up to us straight away.

'My two best readers,' Liz said. 'And I didn't even know you knew each other.'

I looked at the two of them. And I didn't even know *they* knew each other.

'I've kept that book you were asking about, Miranda,' Liz said. 'I'll just go and get it.'

Liz was choosing books for Miranda too now? I followed her up to the counter to check what it was. *The Women in Shakespeare's Plays*. I read the title upside down as Liz handed it over. It was a thick, academic looking book.

'Bet that hasn't got many pictures,' I said but Miranda just ignored me.

'Second best bed,' I said.

Miranda started flicking through the pages.

'He left his wife his second best bed in his will,' I said. 'Guess he didn't think much of women. Or maybe just her.'

'Is that all you know about him?' she asked.

'Well, no. *Nothing will come of nothing*,' I intoned dramatically.

'Give me strength,' Miranda said, but at least she was talking now. 'Some of us actually want to learn useful things. Stretch our minds.'

'*Think again*,' I continued.

Liz came up then. 'Got one for you as well, Molly,' she said. 'This is another French writer.'

'Let me see. I love Marguerite Duras,' Miranda said greedily, but I clutched the paperback to my chest.

'No, you're stretching your mind,' I said. 'You learn your useful things and leave me to mine.' I took the book off to my favourite chair. After a while, Miranda came to stand next to me.

'Got bored?' I asked. 'I said you should have got one with pictures.'

'Oh you,' Miranda cooed, but I could tell her heart wasn't in it. 'I've got a customer soon. Are you walking back?'

I looked at my watch. 'I'm just going to stay here for a bit longer,' I said. 'It's cooler here than in the shop.'

It was only half an excuse. Although I was enjoying the library's air conditioning, I'd just read something interesting. What this writer seemed to be saying was that it was impossible to *make* yourself desirable. In fact, often you didn't know what was inside you that another person was going to want. So, although she didn't come out and state this exactly, what I guessed you had to do was to put everything you had out on display, otherwise you could walk past Mr Right and run the risk of him not noticing the big arrow saying you were for him.

Or something like that.

The girl in the book Liz had given me really put it out there by wearing a big hat and gold shoes. Everyone noticed those so of course the hero spotted her too, but I'd taken to wearing black cover-up clothes from the charity shops. I couldn't help but wonder what it was inside me that Tim had spotted.

As I sat down to read the book, I looked round the library for other clues as to what would make people noticeable. The middle-aged woman browsing the biography shelves was wearing heels so high she had to rest her foot half-out of them when she wasn't walking. The dark haired woman in the children's section had almost black lipstick. The teenage boy looking through the sports bit was carrying a basketball. I looked round for Liz.

She was talking to the man who'd once complained about the lack of a *Daily Telegraph*. I got ready to rescue her.

'But I don't know how to bloody use a computer,' he said as I came up. 'And what's more I'm not going to learn. You can't make me.'

I took a step back. He looked smaller somehow today, and I didn't want to see him humiliated by Liz's sharp tongue.

'Shall we see about that?' she said, but although the words they both used were severe, their manner wasn't. Liz was only looking at him with half her face for a start, turning the other half over to her shoulder as if she really was asking him a question, but then she saw me and straightened up.

'Molly,' she said. 'How's it going? Your friend Miranda's a clever one, isn't she? And what about you? Did today's French goddess have a certain *je ne sais quoi*?'

She sounded as if she thought it was all silly, and sure enough the *Daily Telegraph* man smiled at me indulgently.

'I'll come back later,' I said pointedly. 'When you're not so busy with other customers.'

'No need,' the man said. 'I'm just going. Thanks for the help, Liz.'

We both watched him go. Liz was absent-mindedly stamping the pad in front of her with the date stamp. I thought about her comment about French goddesses.

'He's nice,' I said. 'And he likes you.'

She stamped a bit harder. 'Now don't be silly. He's just a customer. We have to be polite.'

'No,' I said. 'There was something else, like electricity between you. He really really liked you. It was as if no one else in this library existed for him.'

There was hardly an inch of the pad that Liz had left un-inked now. 'Really?' she asked.

'Oh yes,' I said. 'You can always tell. But he's such a gentleman I bet he'll leave it up to you to do the running. He'd never do anything if he thought you might not like it. With someone like that, you'd have to make it clear that you were interested.'

And then I left too, even though I knew Liz wanted me to stay to talk about this more. I was still smiling by the time I got back to the shop but then the torpor of the afternoon quiet got to me. I busied myself tidying up the already immaculate shelves but it was a relief when Mr Roberts finally shut up shop and I could disappear up to my room. I threw myself on the bed and wept until I was spent, and then I thrust my face deep into my pillow. Something sharp dug into my cheek. It was my bag. I pulled out my book, turned to a page at random and began to read.

You don't have to love me. I have love enough for both of us. Just do with me what you will.

No fuss, no bother. Maybe this was the message I'd been waiting for. Although of course I'd rather Tim did love me. Love me so much it hurt him. I washed my face with cold water in the sink downstairs and let myself out of the shop to go and see if he was still waiting for me at the park. Don't ask me how I knew he'd be there, but I did. *Do with me what you will but do love me. Just love me as I love you.* Of course this is what Tim had seen in me.

I wanted Tim to do with me what he would. And that was how I was going to get him to love me as I did him. Or something like that.

Actually I just hoped he'd kiss me. It had been a long time since I'd had a taste of melon.

TWENTY-EIGHT

The next day Miranda was staring fixedly at the shop mannequin in the window of the boutique as I walked up to her.

'Fancy yourself in that?' I asked. The display was summer-themed, designed around tennis. Bright yellow balls were scattered on the floor, giant cut-out rackets were hung from the ceiling as if in disembodied mid-shot. The clothes were all tiny white sleeve-less and halter-necked dresses that looked more like handkerchiefs for women our size.

Miranda gave me a tight half-smile that didn't reach the rest of her face.

'Hello stranger,' I said. 'I came round to the salon yesterday evening for you to do my hair, but you'd gone out. The girls said you were being all mysterious.'

'Just went to see a friend,' she said and I was surprised to feel a sharp pang of jealousy.

'Which friend?' I asked.

Miranda was puffing at her cigarette in this way she had. She always held the butt between her thumb and index-finger so the rest of her hand formed a tunnel for the smoke to travel through.

'Do you care?' she asked.

'What?' I was about to complain that this was unfair and our friendship was more important to me than that, when I remembered talking to Tim in the park that night. 'Only you,' I'd told him. 'I don't have any other friends but you.'

'Have you lost weight?' I knew whatever happened Miranda wouldn't be able to resist talking about her unsuccessful diets.

I was right. She brightened up immediately. 'I have not,' she said firmly, 'and yet do you want to know what I've been eating – or not eating, I should say – recently?'

I didn't particularly, but I was prepared to listen when she told me. Instead though she looked me up and down.

'Although I must say you're the one that's getting thin,' she said. 'Come home with me now and have a decent meal. No excuses. Mum won't mind.'

She was changing, Miranda. She read her magazines less so she didn't have so many tales of misery to tell. Even her clothes were more businesslike. I felt sad for the way she'd stopped coo-ing so much and had started saying things like: 'If I can be direct' or 'I know you won't mind me saying.'

These days you did what Miranda suggested, so an hour later I was sitting in her front room. It was so hot I couldn't stop my eyes drooping. When I opened them though I could tell by the way Miranda's parents were smiling at me that I must have been like that for some time. I shook my head and grinned back. I'd learnt by now that it was always better to join in the joke. Much safer to be seen to be part of the pack.

'You were miles away, hen,' Mrs Bartlett said.

'Welcome back to the land of the half-living.' Mr Bartlett shook his head, and poured himself some more tea. His wheelchair was pushed right up next to the table, a tartan blanket tucked tightly round his legs. I'd noticed already that the one slipper poking out beneath the cover was on the wrong foot. It gave him an even more lopsided look than he had already.

'Manners. Don't just help yourself,' Mrs Bartlett reminded him, and she winked at me. 'I'm sure Molly here could do with something else to eat. You look tired out.'

'Boyfriend keeping her up, I shouldn't wonder.' Mr Bartlett laughed so loudly at his own joke that he choked on the mouthful of cake he'd just taken and had to be patted on the back by Mrs Bartlett. She hit him much harder than was really needed, smiling all the time. When she put a glass of water up to his lips for him to drink, I noticed she thrust the rim against his mouth, clinking it on his teeth. He pushed her arm away in annoyance, catching her on the shoulder so she winced.

Miranda was the only one not joining in the fun.

'Mum was just asking about your parents,' she said. 'Before you fell asleep.'

I concentrated hard on peeling the chocolate icing off the slice of cake I'd just been given. When I raised my head, Mrs Bartlett looked away quickly. Mr Bartlett was fussing with his handkerchief, wiping the water from his face where it had spilt. Only Miranda was still staring at me.

'I told Mum about how your father has to go abroad often for his work,' she said, 'and all the lovely presents he brought you back when you were a kiddie. I'd so much like to see your collection of dolls in foreign costumes. More than a hundred, isn't it Molly?'

I didn't think Miranda had listened to me when I told her all this one night when she was blow-drying my hair. She hadn't asked anything, hadn't made any comment. Just started telling me one of her magazine stories instead.

Mrs Bartlett sighed. 'Lovely,' she repeated, and I had a sudden pang of longing. It felt so safe sitting there in Miranda's sitting room that I was just opening my mouth to tell them how I didn't really have any dolls, when Mrs Bartlett suddenly leant forward. 'But I'd like to hear about this boyfriend too, Molly,' she said. 'Miranda says she hasn't met him, but in my experience – and I did have a fair bit of experience before I met Miranda's father – girls like to talk about their young men.'

I could feel myself blushing, and sure enough, Mrs Bartlett clapped her hands in delight. 'See, Miranda,' she said. 'I told you Molly wouldn't mind. She's not like you, so secretive all of a sudden. Rushing out without so much as a pipsqueak's notice. All those letters you keep getting that you won't let us see. Hushed phone calls you think we don't hear.'

A flush started to creep up Miranda's neck. What did she have to be secretive about? I stored this one away to think about later.

'So tell us all about him,' Mrs Bartlett said.

'He's called Tim and he's perfect.'

'And does he have a job?' she asked.

A few weeks ago even I would have enjoyed explaining in detail about Tim's work as a special adviser but recently he had drummed it into me about how I couldn't tell anyone.

'No,' I said.

Mrs Bartlett looked embarrassed. 'Well, never mind, dear,' she said. 'We can't all be lucky.'

I turned away, but Mrs Bartlett seemed to take my silence as a sign she'd upset me. She rushed round clearing up the cake plates and took them through to the kitchen. Just as Miranda and I looked up at each other, she came back for the teapot. To freshen it, she said, holding it out at arm's length as if it was the teapot that had committed the indiscretion of making me admit Tim didn't have a job. Mr Bartlett had fallen asleep in his wheelchair next to me. Miranda put one finger to her lips to make sure I kept quiet and then silently stood up and wheeled him away from us.

'I'm glad you came, Molly,' she whispered.

'So am I.'

'And now I know you won't mind me saying this but I want to have a word about your hair.' Miranda looked concerned.

I put my hand up automatically and was surprised to feel how greasy it was.

'So how about if you come up to my bedroom now and I sort you out properly?' Miranda said. 'Maybe I could even find you a nice outfit I don't want any more. I'd love to see you in something bright and youthful.'

I watched Miranda's bum as she climbed the stairs in front of me. She'd got changed into something comfortable the minute we'd got to her house, and the material on her 'bright and youthful' leggings was stretched so the colours across her thighs were more like random impressionist streaks than the colourful flowers they were supposed to be.

'So what did you have in mind for me to wear then?' I asked as she opened her bedroom door. Miranda's home was so much like ones I used to dream of having when I was a child, that for some reason, I been expecting a little girl's bedroom too. Pink princess style, with fairy lights and fluffy cushions. I couldn't speak when I saw inside. The walls were painted light green and she had wooden shutters at her windows. The linen on her bed was plain white, the cotton so soft and luxurious you felt comforted just running your fingers along it. The furniture all matched, but not in a just-bought-at-a-large-Swedish-style-warehouse way. The carpet was straw matting, and she had just two pictures on the walls – black and white posters of old movie stars. Of course, this was just what I would have done with my room at her age if I had lived the perfect life. I looked at Miranda.

'You know your cheekbones remind me a little of hers,' I said, pointing to the photograph of Katharine Hepburn.

Miranda smiled and moved a pile of books off her dressing table so I could sit down in front of the mirror. I watched as she pulled off the rubber band and my hair came tumbling down to

133

my shoulders. She sprayed some dry shampoo all over and started brushing it out.

'So tell me about your dad,' I asked. 'Did he lose his foot in an accident?'

'He ran over himself.'

I turned round so she had to stop brushing my hair. 'Get away with you.'

Miranda sighed. 'It was a new automatic car. He put it into reverse, but then remembered he needed to get something out of the boot so he nipped round the back just as it started to move. He'd forgotten that automatics keep going.'

She said it without feeling, and in a way I guessed she'd rehearsed because there was no room for sympathy in her account, or laughter either.

'And that's why you and your mum have to look after him all the time?' I asked. 'Can't he do anything for himself now?'

Miranda started frizzing my hair out around my head. 'He hasn't changed that much,' she said. 'He did sod all before too, but that's men for you, isn't it?'

'My dad . . .' I started.

'Yes?'

This was something new. It was the first time I started talking about the past and Miranda hadn't shut me up. In fact her interest was all but crackling through the brush and on to my hair but I was too psyched up to tell my story to wonder what had changed.

'He was a bit of a bully really. He was always thinking the worst of me. He never let me do anything that the other girls were allowed to do. I think he wanted me kept innocent for ever.'

Miranda nodded, but didn't say anything. The silence began to be uncomfortable.

'Can I go on?' I asked. 'Shall I tell you more?'

'Please,' Miranda said. She was brushing my hair gently now.

'He was always taking centre stage,' I said. 'It was like he always had to be the only one anyone in the room looked at. My mum just did whatever he said. I couldn't work out why she put up with it.'

'My mum hates my dad.'

I thought back to the scene I'd witnessed downstairs. Miranda was probably right. So there could be trouble even in paradise? Miranda smoothed my hair down, and I relaxed into the feeling of being looked after.

'He used to do this thing,' I said. 'He'd lie in bed as if he was dead and I'd have to sit by him, hold his hand and tell him how much I loved him. And then just when I started to get teary, he'd jump up suddenly and give me the shock of my life. I was only about nine the first time, but we carried on until . . .' I paused. 'Until it was the only way we could be nice to each other, I suppose. The rest of the time it was as if we were in some kind of battle. A fight to the death. Every weapon allowed.'

'Men,' Miranda said, curling the ends of my hair under neatly. 'They're just kids really. I suppose he thought he was being funny.'

I considered this. I'd expected Miranda to react in horror like the biology teacher and the counsellor, but now I remembered how it was always me asking him to play dead like that. The anticipation of not knowing when he was going to jump up would make me teary with excitement, not sorrow or fear. It was a way of briefly controlling the fear that was always around him. Perhaps I even relished the chance to tell him how much I loved him. 'You're probably right,' I said finally. 'I hadn't thought of it like that before. Although—'

'There,' Miranda cut me off mid-sentence, taking a step back from me and pointing at my reflection. 'Doesn't that look better?'

I looked at myself in the mirror; my hair was hanging down

on either side of my face like curtains I longed to draw as if I could shut myself off. I nodded, numb.

'But you still look awful peaky, Molly. Do you want to stay here tonight? Have some supper in front of the TV with us?'

But I'd had enough confessing for now. I liked talking about Dad so much I was worried I wouldn't know when to stop. And I knew how dangerous that was. Plus speaking to Miranda had given me a new slant on things. One I wanted to think about. 'I'll just get home.'

Miranda started rooting around in her wardrobe and I thought I'd upset her again, but she was beaming when she turned, a stiff black cardboard bag in her hand.

'Here we go,' she said. I went over to stand next to her as she undid the thick black ribbon that tied the bag together. She wound the ribbon round her fingers, leaving it coiled up by the side. Inside the bag, there were layers of black tissue paper, which she pulled out carefully, smoothing each piece down with her podgy fingers, folding it up and placing it on the bed.

Not even this performance prepared me for the dress Miranda finally took out. It was peach pink, a shiny slip of a garment that seemed to move through Miranda's fingers like water. When she held it up, I could see the gathers at the neck, the silver straps that made the dress look as if it wasn't stable enough to stand up on its own. I'd never seen anything quite so perfect.

Miranda held it in front of her and looked at herself in the mirror. We were both silent, full of a painful longing.

'I'd never fit into it,' Miranda said eventually. 'And it cost a fortune even in the sale, but I couldn't resist. I get it out sometimes just to look at it. It's French, you know.'

I nodded, unable to take my eyes off the dress. It seemed to throw up a light on to Miranda's face that made her glow.

'It wouldn't fit me either,' I said.

'Would you like to try it on?'

My heart jumped. It was all I could do to stop myself running over and pulling the dress from her, but I had recognised the expression she had on her face when she looked in the mirror. It had been love. She loved that dress, and I knew I shouldn't take it away from her, but she practically forced it into my hands.

'It's your dress,' I said, hardly breathing as I rubbed my fingers up and down the material. I put my face down to smell it, and was surprised to inhale the sweetness of silk. I'd been expecting Chanel perfume, woody cigars, money.

'OK.' Miranda put her arm out for me to drape the dress over. 'If you don't want it.'

Miranda's three dolls were sitting on top of the wardrobe. They were the sort of dolls you don't play with, staring down at me with their horrible lifelike expressions, the frills and patterns of their period costumes mocking the perfect simplicity of both Miranda's dress and the room they sat in.

'I do want it,' I gulped. No zip or buttons, just a thin ribbon tie at the neck. I adjusted the straps, pulled the belt in at my waist, felt my breasts and stomach with my fingertips as if I could mould the dress to my skin.

'Lovely,' Miranda said, sitting down on the bed and watching me. 'I knew it would be just right for you.'

'Lovely.' I gazed at myself in the mirror. This was the Molly I always knew was hidden inside. Beautiful. For a moment I wished my father could see me now. He'd see it was all right to let me grow up.

I wore the dress home under my coat. Never mind that my trainers and ankle socks were sticking out underneath. There was no way I was going to take it off. 'Are you sure you want to give it to me?' I'd kept asking Miranda until she said if I asked her again, she'd take it back. 'Just a loan,' I said then, 'until you lose enough weight for it to fit you too. I really do think you're looking thinner.'

'Bye, Molly,' she said, putting her hand on my shoulder and steering me out of the door. I hadn't said goodbye to her parents. Miranda said she didn't want her mum to see the dress as it would only provoke questions.

'I've had a happy time,' I told Miranda, 'such a happy time.' And it was true. I hadn't been in too many houses like Miranda's. Ones that felt like real homes. Where people could bicker, even hate each other, and yet it didn't seem to matter. Fear didn't underline everything. It was just how I imagined. I all but skipped down the street, only keeping away from car lights when I remembered Tim's instructions. It was hard to stay hidden though, when what I really wanted was for everyone to look at me. Even if they couldn't see the dress through the coat, its magic must be obvious.

You see, there was something else too. When I'd looked in the mirror, it was the first time I'd seen a resemblance to my mother. I was a younger version maybe. But still a version.

TWENTY-NINE

Four more ribbons were hanging on the tree, one of them threaded through a pink cardboard heart. There was still no visible reason why this was happening.

Seeing the decorations silenced my usual conversations with Jessica. I filled up the water bottle I'd brought up with me, sprinkled water on the pansies I'd planted, clipping off the dead flowers with my fingers and scattering the wilted petals round the edge of the bench. It was if she wasn't mine any more, the ribbons a reminder that I was just an interloper on her bench.

SEIZE THE DAY.

But could I, even with the dress?

By the time Tim came, I was skittish with nerves. I didn't want to sit there any more.

'But where shall we go?' Tim asked.

I realised I had no idea what to expect from him any more. He looked younger tonight, his face no longer set and square as it got at times. When I reached to take his hand, he just held mine softly before putting it up to his mouth and kissing it in the way I didn't have to ask him for any more. Then he closed my fingers one by one around the spot he'd just kissed.

'Molly,' he said.

'Tim,' I replied.

Then he pressed my hand tight. 'Keep it safe,' he said. 'For when times aren't so good.'

Although Tim was so thin, he was tall and large framed. I saw now that my fist fitted into his hand easily. It made me feel small and light in spirit. As playful as a kid.

'We could go to the pub,' I suggested.

Tim shook his head. 'They're full of people.'

'Isn't that the point?'

Then Tim did a strange thing. He kept on shaking his head, swinging it over from side to side. Any dreams I might have had of getting him to wear tailored rugby shirts and sitting in the pub with me were fading quickly, but I still wanted to get away from the bench.

'Shall we go and see our bear?' I suggested. We'd been back to the department store twice since just to stand there gazing at each other's distorted reflections through the clean glass of the bear's belly.

'Not today,' Tim said. 'It's too hot.'

'Let's just go back to my room,' I said, 'and we can decide what to do.'

On the way there, Tim made me walk a few steps in front of him. I kept turning round and pretending not to notice him, but he didn't find it as funny as me so after a while, I just stopped dead and waited for him to crash into me instead. Probably because the whole thing was so absurd, I had a picture from one of those old black and white Keystone Cops films in my head, the one where a line of policemen concertina into each other. Tim stayed behind me though, his hands resting lightly on my shoulders to keep me still.

'Did you see something?' he whispered. 'Is someone there?'

'Yes,' I lied, my voice as close to an urgent whisper as I could make it. 'There was someone in a long coat and a big hat. He's just slipped into that alley, but he'd been watching us. I'm sure of that.'

Tim tutted. 'I should have seen him,' he said. 'What's wrong with me?'

'What shall we do?' I took the opportunity to pretend to be frightened and snuggle up to Tim. He pushed me away, but gently. He was looking this way and that down the empty street.

'Just run to the shop,' he whispered. 'Shut the door but leave it on the latch. I'll be up soon, just got some things to sort out here first.'

I ran, but not before stealing a quick kiss from him because I was being so brave. I tried for one more, pushing into him in the hope he'd forget about the phantom stalker and concentrate on me instead, but he whispered that I had to go. He'd never forgive himself if anything happened to me.

'But you'll come soon,' I begged. This joke wasn't going at all how I had expected. Instead of the frisson I'd hoped for, I could just see Tim disappearing on another wild-goose chase.

A middle-aged commuter was walking past us now, his face grey and drained of energy, a heavy briefcase weighing him down on one side. Tim must have used the distraction to slink to the edge of the pavement, because although I swore that I never took my eyes off him, he suddenly vanished as more people started to appear, walking on their own or in groups of twos and threes. One of the city trains must have just come in.

Despite myself, I was shaking as I went into the shop, turning my head round several times to make sure no one was following me. Up in my room, I sat on the bed, my hands on my knees, staring at the door as I waited for Tim.

Fifteen minutes later, I was still watching as I saw the handle turn and the door started opening slowly. The thumping of my heart must have been blotted out the sound of his steps on the stairs.

'Are you OK?' I asked. 'What happened?'

Tim was breathing heavily as if he'd been running as he came to sit next to me. 'I think it's time I told you everything, Molly,' he said. 'But you must promise never ever to breathe a word to anyone, no matter what they promise. Or threaten.'

I pulled my hair over to cover my face, holding it down with my palms flat. Tim peeled my hands away. 'Do you promise?' he repeated, but even as I nodded and although this was what I wanted, I was so scared I might burst from all the untold and untellable stories that were filling me up already.

'Are you sure?' he said, and I nodded again but then, as I listened to him speak, I felt my eyes get heavy and start to close, my body sink into his. I pinched at myself to try to keep awake until finally giving up all urge to fight, I let him talk me gently to sleep.

When I woke, it was morning and Tim was gone.

142

Liz was on her knees over in the biography section. I stood behind and coughed several times. She was trying to ram a book into a gap half its size, so she looked irritated when she first glanced up. Then she did a double take.

'Molly May,' she said. 'Just look at you.'

I laughed. 'It's Miranda's dress,' I said. 'She gave it to me. Do you like it?' I shook my hair out as I pirouetted for her, like they did in the shampoo advertisements.

'I do.' She stood up, but not before dropping the thick tome she'd been holding on top of the bookcase. 'It's only that footballer's book,' she explained. 'It's so popular that every time I put it back, someone only takes it out again. Hardly worth the effort. So, what brought this on then?'

'Miranda didn't want it any more.'

Liz put her hands on my shoulders and turned her head round this way and that to study me closely.

'It's not just the dress though,' she said. 'Have you lost weight as well?'

'A little.'

'More than a little. You're half the person you were.'

There were no scales at the stationery shop, and the ones in the swimming pool were too public, so I hadn't weighed myself since the doctor's appointment my mother made me have. It felt like years ago. I pinched my skin round my waist. Yes, definitely much tighter. How had I missed that?

'You're becoming a real little eye-popper,' Liz said. 'I suppose this is all down to the new man?'

I nodded. 'I think it might be.'

'Young love,' Liz said. 'Mind you, old love isn't so bad either. It's like getting on a bicycle. You suddenly remember how much you enjoy the ride, if you know what I mean.' She laughed her dirty laugh, so I smiled politely along with her although I didn't like it when she spoke like this. It wasn't how I saw the story going.

'So aren't you going to ask me then?' she said after a pause. 'You know, about the man you said was a little bit keen on me. He's a retired accountant, I'll have you know. I wouldn't have to worry about pensions if I ended up with him.'

I snorted.

'You may laugh, young lady,' Liz said, 'but one day you'll realise there's more to life than flowers and kisses. Give me a man who knows his DOW index from his G-strings any day.'

'But you're always telling me love is what's important,' I said. I might have temporarily forgotten about my plans for Liz, but I did know pensions weren't quite what I had in mind. 'Money doesn't matter if you've got each other.'

To my relief, Liz suddenly smiled, her shoulders relaxed down. 'And when you're your age so that's just how it should be, young Molly. I wouldn't have done any of this without you. You've given me a new lease of life. Come and tell me what your Romeo thinks of his new-look Juliet. It's time for my coffee break anyway.'

So I went into Liz's office and told her a story all about how Tim and I had gone to a pub and he'd got jealous because everyone had looked at me. I told her how we talked and talked until late, and how I'd listened to every word he said. How we shared all our secrets. There wasn't anything I couldn't tell him.

'It must be like that for you,' I said. 'With your accountant.'

She took my hand and stroked it. 'Enjoy this, Molly. Enjoy every minute because, I promise you, nothing in books is anything like as good as your life right now.'

I wasn't used to seeing Liz like this. She looked as if she was going to cry. I felt ashamed for her.

'So tell me all about the accountant,' I said.

'He's called Bob,' she shrugged. 'Oh, he'll do, but he's nothing like you and your boy really. No point pretending otherwise when you get to my age.'

'I think it's so romantic,' I lied. 'It's like you've waited all your life for The One, and now he's walked into your library and found you.'

Liz stared at me for a second, and then stood up. 'Must get on,' she said firmly. 'God knows what havoc those customers will have got up to while we've been nattering. Putting S's back in the C's, I shouldn't be surprised, and other heinous crimes.'

After she'd gone, I took our cups over to the small corner sink to rinse them through, and stood there letting the hot water wash over my hands until it became too hot to bear. I wiped my hands dry carefully. The skin was red and warm with lies.

When I went back into the main library though, Bob had come in and was leaning over the counter chatting to Liz. I watched them together for a bit. It didn't look as if she was just making do the way she smiled and laughed quietly, nothing like the normal Liz-roar, when he was speaking. And then when he leant across the counter and gently pushed a lock of her hair away from her eye, she just put her head down and rested it gently on his hand. It was a gesture almost too tender to watch.

I didn't bother with hot water any more when I took a shower at the leisure centre. Just went straight to cold, as icily sharp as I could bear. I timed myself, forcing myself to stay in each time for longer and longer. My whole body smarted as the water hit it; the hairs on my legs, arms, stomach, standing up to attention during the onslaught.

And then one day, as I was getting changed there was a scream from the showers. We all rushed through.

A woman emerged from one of the cubicles, covering her body with her arms before she picked up her towel and started rubbing herself dry.

'The shower must be broken,' she said. 'The water's freezing. It gave me quite a shock.'

We all laughed with relief. Bathed ourselves in the warm glow of comfort in our smiles, and I had a clear moment when I saw what it would be like for everything to be all right.

THIRTY-ONE

Mr Roberts had a new purple cardigan. He tried to pretend it was an old one that had been knocking around for ages, but then, when I was nipping through to the kitchen to make some coffee, I caught him studying his reflection in the little mirror there.

'Very smart,' I said. 'So who you are trying to impress?'

'It's Mrs Roberts,' he said, lifting his glasses up to take a closer look at himself. 'She's insisting it's too draughty for me here. I can't seem to shift this sickness. But a cardigan! I thought she was joking at first. I should have known better.'

'What's wrong with a cardigan?' I laughed.

'It's a bit pansy,' he said. 'But there's no telling her that, of course.'

'French people are bound to see clothes a bit differently.'

Mr Roberts nodded, pulling down the waistband in front of him so the front was almost concave. It seemed I wasn't the only one to be losing weight. 'You're right, Molly. Do you know her brother wears pink shirts? Pink! What do you think about that then?'

He folded his arms and I shook my head as if in disbelief. It was nice to be talking together like this.

'And once he wore a yellow tie, and these cufflinks in the shape of enamel flowers. I don't mind telling you it made my blood boil. All those starving kids in the world, and a man's spending his money prettifying himself with flowers. It's just not right.' He shook his head.

'Poor kids,' he repeated. 'Poor little blighters.'

I wanted to encourage him to talk more about the clothes and less about the poor children. I was worried that it would bring back memories of Leanne and he'd have me up that ladder before I knew it. 'Tell me about Mrs Roberts's family,' I asked. 'What was it like to grow up in France? It must have been exciting for her.'

It was the mid-morning lull in the shop so I figured I had nothing to lose by trying to talk normally with him. Besides, Mr Roberts had changed recently. He didn't find fault so often and was more likely to let me speak. At first, I thought it was because Mrs Roberts praised me, but then I noticed he was like that with customers too. He was spending time with the actual people who came into the shop, not just the big paper orders. A few days before, he had stood by as a schoolgirl tried out all the scented pens several times over before she finally choose the one she preferred. 'She reminded me of Leanne,' he said defensively, when he caught me staring at him.

I could see what he meant. There was something about the little girl's bunches, her thin legs and red sandals that made me nostalgic too for how life used to be when I first came to his shop. When it was almost exciting to climb the ladder because I wasn't sure what story would come out.

'Have you ever been to France?' I asked him. I couldn't understand why he and Mrs Roberts weren't living there. I would if I were him.

Mr Roberts sat down heavily on the stool that we used half as a kitchen chair, and half for sorting out stock. He fiddled with the buttons of his cardigan. 'Go on then, Molly,' he said, 'I tell you what. You make us a nice strong cup of tea, and you can tell me a story down here in comfort for a change.'

I was just about to say that wasn't fair, that I'd been the one asking him for a story, but I caught his face. *Now Molly.*

It was strange telling a story to him when we were on the same level. I stuttered a bit to start with. He tapped his fingers on the table, drumming out his impatience but that just made it worse. Close up, he looked so ill. I couldn't stop looking at the dark circles round his eyes, the high red spots on his cheeks which only accentuated the rest of his deathly pale complexion, the veins on the side of his nose which looked as if they'd been drawn on by purple felt pen.

I breathed in and out deeply. 'OK,' I said. 'Remember I told you about my father and how strict he was.'

Mr Roberts nodded. 'I'm glad Mrs Roberts and I never had children,' he said. 'I couldn't have coped with the responsibility of a girl. Mrs Roberts now, she could have managed anything. I think she might have liked a little one too. She never said anything. Well, she wouldn't, not if she thought it would upset me, but she'd have been a good mum. No doubt about that.' He sighed, and I waited impatiently for him to stop talking about Mrs Roberts. Either he wanted a story from me, or he didn't.

'Well, he had every right to be anxious about me,' I said. 'I was such a bad girl. One night I crept out of bed after everyone was asleep and went off to the park, dressed just in my nightgown. I walked round first of all but then I sat down. I stared at everyone that passed. There were all these men coming out of the pub.'

I paused then. Mr Roberts was drinking his tea carefully, wiping his mouth with his big white handkerchief after each sip. I couldn't think of what to say next. All my thoughts had got stuck somewhere else. My mind was blank. I took a gulp of my tea, cradling the cup with both hands. I wasn't at all sure where this story was going.

'And then all of a sudden I could see someone standing in front of them.' Suddenly my words starting spilling out. 'It was Leanne.'

'Leanne came back!' Mr Roberts looked up so quickly, he

missed his mouth and tea drops splattered his chin. I looked away until he cleaned himself up with his handkerchief. 'I knew she would,' he said. 'Little Leanne.'

'One man came over to me. He asked me if he could sit next to me on the bench, and I said yes. Stupid of me, I suppose. Leanne put her finger up to her lips so I'd keep her being there a secret. He didn't seem to see her, but I could feel her there. When she crept round behind us, she pressed my shoulder gently as she passed.

'And then just before the man reached out to start touching me, Leanne climbed over and put herself between me and him,' I said. 'It was so dark he couldn't have noticed. I just felt her back pressed against me. When he hugged her too tight, her gasp went through me too. I pulled my nightgown back down over my knees, protecting myself, making sure he couldn't touch me, but Leanne didn't seem to mind.'

Mr Roberts put his hand up to his chest. His fingers started scrabbling at his shirt buttons. 'Did he hurt her?' he asked.

I could picture the scene exactly. The smell of wood and blood and Leanne's lemony hint of fear. In front of me, Mr Roberts had his head down, and I was just about to check he really was all right when the shop bell went and a customer came in. I tried to look sorry, but I was out of that kitchen like a flash. The truth was it was a relief to escape. The story had got ahead of me and I didn't know what I'd say if I stayed there. I put on a bright smile to greet the customer but Tim was standing in front of the counter instead.

'Am I pleased to see you,' I said.

'I don't know. Are you?' He looked puzzled and just a bit worried. Or perhaps it was partly the effect of the suit he was wearing. Not one of those ill-fitting, awkward suits the boys at school used to wear for weddings and special dos but a proper work suit, with a striped shirt and tie. He even had a battered brown briefcase with him.

'I can't have any time off right now,' I said. 'But I'm finishing in about an hour. Do you want to wait in my room, or shall we meet in the park later?'

Tim was shuffling round the displays, picking up pens and putting them down, flicking his fingers through the envelopes. All with the one hand. His other was gripping his bag so tightly his knuckles were blanched. When he came to stand before me I noticed he was rocking backwards and forwards on his soles.

'Molly,' he said, and then he took my hand, raised it to his lips and kissed my palm, shutting my fingers round the spot in that way he had.

'Tim.' I indicated towards the kitchen with my head, grimacing to show that Mr Roberts was there and we couldn't really talk now.

'I've just come for my words anyway,' he said. 'It won't take long.'

'What words?'

'Don't mess, Molly. I'm tired. I wasn't really thinking about what I was doing when I told you everything. It was unfair of me, so if you just give it all back then we can carry on like before.'

It was only when I took one step back from him that I noticed how quickly my heart was beating. I stared at him.

He tapped his briefcase and gave me a quizzical smile. 'You do still have it all, don't you?' he asked. 'You haven't given it to anyone else yet.'

'I haven't told anyone anything,' I said, but when he moved to take my hand again, I snatched it away. 'Is this a joke?'

Tim sighed.

We'd just taken a delivery of two office chairs in the shop. They were sitting by the window, still covered in their plastic wrapping, their backs facing each other as if they were having a conversation. Tim went to sit on the blue one and swivelled from one side to the other, looking out at the street. I still felt frightened although I could hear Mr Roberts coughing in the kitchen. It was a dry, sore-sounding cough and then there was the noise of a tap running. He must have been getting himself a glass of water to soothe his throat.

I went over to where Tim was sitting. He spun round so he was looking up at me and then he grabbed me round the waist and thrust his head into my body, but gently, like a lamb looking for its mother. I felt myself soften and respond.

He took hold of my wrists and ran his thumbs along my pulse points. 'What will I do?' he said. 'How am I going to admit that I've given everything away to you? I don't know what's happening to me.'

I could have told him then that I'd been asleep the whole time, but something stopped me. 'I'll forget it all,' I said grandly. I spoke in a high-pitched childish accent to show him I was joking.

Tim didn't smile. We were both looking out of the window at the grey street now. The sky had that dark, threatening air that comes before heavy summer rain and the few passers-by seemed to be rushing to get inside. Because of the shape of the glass, our reflections seemed to be smaller versions of ourselves. Children holding hands to copy their parents.

'Or I could recruit you, I suppose,' Tim said. 'But there are risks. We'd have to spend a lot of time together on the preparations.'

The surge of excitement I felt was tempered by the noise of Mr Roberts coughing again in the kitchen. I wondered if I should go and check everything was all right, but I wanted to stay with Tim.

'I'd like that,' I said.

'It's not a game, you can't decide just like that,' Tim said. 'There's a long hard concentrated training programme ahead of us. You'll have to think hard, Molly, because your life won't be the same again.'

'Good,' I said. I was ready for another change. Once you've thrown away everything, it's easier to start again. And again. 'When can we start?'

We arranged to meet on the bench that evening.

Tim left his briefcase behind when he left. I was just putting the chairs back when I noticed it. By the time I rushed out to try to catch him, the street was empty apart from one short, round man who was holding a newspaper above his head as he ran. The rain was lashing down, puddles already starting to form. I stared closely at the rushing figure. Tim had said I could begin my training by practising watching skills. Would I be able to identify this man if I came across him again and he didn't have that paper over him? I was just screwing up my eyes to study him better when he dashed down one of the alleys. Maybe I'd be better starting off with inanimate objects.

A Coke bottle was lying in the gutter; a red car parked by the café; an empty carrier bag blew wetly down the street.

Over at the hairdressing salon, a huddle of women were standing round the doorway. They must have been waiting for the rain to subside so they wouldn't ruin their new hairstyles. I waved in the general direction in case Miranda was watching, but then dropped my arm sharply. Tim had said not to draw attention to myself. This was going to be harder than I thought. I went back into the shop and shut the door.

'It's pouring out there,' I called out to Mr Roberts. 'Finally. The rain's been a long time coming. Shall I make us another cup of tea? I can't imagine we're going to have too many customers this afternoon.'

I was still talking when he came through from the kitchen with his coat already on and buttoned up. The shadows under his eyes seemed to be getting darker and heavier. When I stood next to him, I wasn't sure if he'd shrunk or I'd grown. He was shaking slightly and I wanted to put my hand out to steady him.

'Are you off now?' I asked. 'Why don't you wait until the rain's finished?'

Just then, a maroon car drove up to the front door, dipping its headlights. 'You'll be all right for the rest of the afternoon, won't you?' Mr Roberts asked. 'I rang Mrs Roberts and asked her to pick me up. I'm not feeling too good. You can shut up shop. Maybe that's better than you having to take all that responsibility.'

'Mr Roberts?'

When he turned round, I could see how impatient he was to leave.

'It wasn't my story that's troubled you, was it? You're all right, aren't you?'

He nodded, but his shoulders were hunched and he didn't want to look at me. Leanne was all right, she told the men to eff off, I wanted to shout after him, but the words didn't come. After he'd gone, I turned the shop sign round to 'Closed' and took Tim's briefcase up to my room and laid it in the middle of the bed. I wouldn't put it past Tim for this to be a challenge he'd set for me. Would it be a good thing or a bad thing to rifle through his papers? He hadn't even told me who we were working for, or what we were going to be doing.

Picking the case up again, I went over to the mirror. I practised holding it down by my side, and then up in front of my face, shielding my nose and mouth so only my eyes were visible. It was surprisingly heavy. I weighed it first in one hand and then the other. Then I put it under the bed, pushing it with my foot so it was well hidden.

It was four o'clock. I had about two hours to kill before I could go across and see Miranda, three hours before Tim normally came to the park. I went to sit by the window and watched the rain-drops chase each other down the glass, following their crooked progress with my finger, tapping whenever they stopped as if I could control their progress. Below, the shop lights gave the street an almost festive air. The rain was slowly stopping, and people were venturing out. I could see the tops of umbrellas weaving their way along, jerking this way and that like brightly coloured circles.

I stretched out both arms, put my palms flat, my forehead resting against the cold glass. No one ever looked up, but if they had they would have seen a picture of utter despair. I wondered if they might think I'd been kidnapped, what sort of stories they would go home and tell their families about me. I thought about Leanne and how nice it had felt when I told the story of how she'd rescued me in the park.

That gave me an idea. I went downstairs and found the yellow pencil case I'd kept safe below the till, and filled it with pens and pencils from the displays. Then I got a lined pad and started to write.

> *I am being treated as a*
> *slave. They will not let*
> *me free. Please rescue me.*

I tore off the piece of paper, folded it with knife-edge precision and stuck it between the notebooks. Then I wrote on the next sheet.

> *Do not try to talk to me direct*
> *as you will just make it worse*
> *but I need help. Call the police*
> *immediately.*

This one I folded into a tiny square and popped it into the box for one of the printers we'd just had delivered.

For the third one I just wrote two words:

HELP ME!

And then I stuffed the note down the side of a red plastic pencil case which I took care to place visibly back on the display.

THIRTY-TWO

The rain emphasised the smell of autumn coming. It was rich in the air, although the flowers were still putting on a brave show. I was sitting on the bench looking at the latest crop of ribbons and hearts on the tree when Tim came up behind me.

'So did you see me this time?'

'Yes.'

'You can't have.' He sat next to me, the picture of disappointment.

'I watched you,' I said. 'You started off there.' I pointed out the entrance to the park where he'd come in. 'And then you went to that tree, and then that one, and then you ran over there, stood still a while and came here.'

'Shit.' His head fell down to his chest.

'But I knew you were there, Tim. Maybe I wouldn't have noticed anything if I hadn't been looking out for you.'

'Maybe.'

I spread my coat out to give him something dry to sit on. He folded his arms around his thin T-shirt, his long legs crossed in front of him so I could see his ankles. I rubbed my hand flat along his thighs, feeling the rough denim against my palm, and then rested my head on his shoulder.

'Do you want to have a go now?' Tim asked. 'You can walk round the back to start with so I won't know where you're coming from.'

'Not really.'

There was a group of teenagers celebrating something under one of the trees on the other side of the park. They'd hung some tarpaulin from the branches to make a tent, had lit a fire to sit round and one of them had a bongo drum on which he was just tapping away quietly.

'We can work on your identity then,' Tim said. He reached up and twirled a strand of my hair round his fingers. 'Could you cut this off?'

I liked my long hair, but I liked sitting there under the canopy of Tim's arm more. If losing my hair was important to him, then that was fine by me. 'Miranda will do it,' I said firmly. I wasn't going to give Tim any reason to doubt me.

'What's the name of your first pet?' he asked.

'Charlie,' I lied. 'Why?'

'And the town you were born in?'

A couple had split away from the teenage group. The guy was leading the girl off by the hand, pulling her into the shadows. I watched them go, hoping she wasn't drunk, that she knew what she was doing and that she wanted to leave the safety of the group. Although they must have been my age, I felt so much older than all of them. The girl stumbled and he dragged her a few steps impatiently.

'Shall we go back to my room?' I said.

'We need a name for you first. Charlie what?'

'You decide.'

Tim pulled me close. I could feel him rubbing his chain against my hair. 'Charlie Canterbury,' he said.

'We should go to the pub and have a proper conversation in the warmth,' I said. 'Get rid of this damp feeling.'

Tim ignored me. 'And you're twenty-five. You work in an office and you live with your mother and father.'

'Not with them,' I said quickly. 'Charlie Canterbury has her own little flat where she does exactly what she wants. And with a roof garden and an outdoor shower,' I added.

'OK,' he laughed. 'And what else does this woman have?'

'Well, it's funny, but there's this strange man she's in love with,' I said.

'Not good,' Tim said. 'We'll have to get rid of him straight away. You can't afford commitments in this game.'

'Now that's a pity.' I looked at Tim. 'Because I'm rather fond of him myself.'

Tim liked the fact that my room had long windows overlooking the street. He pulled a chair up to the window and gave me a running commentary of what was happening down below.

'So Molly.'

I was lying flat on my bed, my hands crossed in front of me. I had my eyes shut, but opened one to look at him.

'You've just failed the test,' Tim said. 'You're Charlie now. Remember?'

I went to sit next to him. He was taking up all the available space on the chair, so after a bit I gave up perching and sat cross legged on the floor, with my back against the side instead.

'What do you like best about me, Tim?' I asked. 'Not the usual, but what do you like about me that you've never liked about anyone else?'

He was silent.

'There must be something,' I said eventually. 'Or is it wrong of me to ask? It's just that it's been puzzling me. Miranda's always saying things like 'that's typical you, Molly', and Mr Roberts too, but what is me? I'm not sure I've ever known. What if you never find out who you are?'

Tim stayed silent. I put my hand up to prod him to make sure he hadn't fallen asleep, but he caught hold of my wrist and tightened his fingers around it slightly. I put my mouth against my upper arm and sucked at it until the skin went red.

'Do you just disappear?' I continued. 'Miranda used to do all these quizzes in her magazines to check whether she's good at work, or in bed, or shopping, but you could lie, couldn't you? You could answer the questions to be anyone you liked. Liz said they had someone at the library who pretended he'd written one of the books there. They even set up a table for him so he could talk to the reading group about his book, but he turned out to be just some random nutter who happened to have the same name as the author. It took them ages to get rid of him. So what's the difference between me and Charlie Canterbury? What do you like better about me than you like about her? What's typical Molly Drayton?'

'Molly's too nice,' Tim mumbled.

'And Charlie's not?'

'Charlie Canterbury is dangerous. She doesn't need anyone else. She's only interested in herself. Molly should watch out for her. That's a message you may like to pass on.'

I twisted my wrist away from Tim, and sat up so I could look at him. It was hard to tell when Tim was just trying to be funny.

'Kiss me,' I said. Sometimes Tim liked me demanding things from him. Other times, though, I'd see him almost physically shrivel, and I'd vow never to do it again. The trouble was that if I didn't take the initiative, nothing would ever happen between us. And however many times I told myself to keep cool, to let Tim take the lead, when I was near him my body started ordering me around in ways I wasn't always sure I wanted to control. It was just what my father must have worried about.

Except, apart from that one time in the shop, Tim had done nothing more than kiss me. Now he started buttoning up his shirt, and searching for his shoes. I slid them towards him.

'I've a meeting in about half an hour,' he said.

'Shall I come?'

'No.'

'Will you tell them about me at least?' I asked.

He paused, and then carried on tucking his shirt into his trousers. 'Of course,' he said. 'You're one of the team now.'

I should have asked for more details then, and it wasn't just that I didn't want to admit I'd fallen asleep. No, if I was honest, I didn't care what team Tim thought I was part of. All I knew was that it meant Tim and I had a reason to be together. And that meant I had a reason for this life I was leading. I was happy as I watched him go. He stayed close to the buildings, his head down. I stared after him until he was out of sight, and then I climbed between the sheets of the bed.

My fingers moved automatically to their normal pinching position, and then almost without me being consciously aware of what was happening, my hand slipped up between my knicker elastic and I rubbed myself gently.

My father would have killed me. Told me I was unnatural, that I was coming to all the bad ends he'd imagined for me, but I kept on. And what did I think of as I made myself come?

I know I did try to picture Tim, but somehow it was Leanne I saw clearest. With my free hand, I clutched at my pillow as I imagined hugging her helpless body tight to me, and then all of a sudden, like a sacrifice, I felt my body swim into hers as I promised to protect her forever, just as she did me. And it was only then that the sweetness of it all finally took over and made me cry. After that it was quickly over.

THIRTY-THREE

When Mrs Roberts came to the shop early the next morning, I was still asleep. I stumbled down the stairs bleary eyed in my Snoopy nightshirt, rubbing my mouth when I heard her shouting from below, and there she was, checking for dust by the desk light display, looking immaculate. The parting in her dark hair was a knife-cut across her white scalp.

'I have come here personally to tell you Mr Roberts is very ill.' No hello or any other greeting.

'I'm sorry.' I pushed my hair behind my ears, trying to look a bit more presentable. She was wearing a maroon suit with big round buttons. Her shoes were high-heeled, black and shiny. My feet were bare and large, and I was conscious of my loose breasts under my nightshirt. I crossed my arms.

'He will not be here today.'

If I was going to get a day off work then Tim and I could do more training. I tried to look upset. 'What's going to happen with the shop?' I asked.

'I'm putting you in charge,' she said.

'Me? Mr Robert's never let me—' I made myself shut up. I didn't want her to change her mind.

'You can do this, yes?' she said.

Too right I could. I couldn't believe it. Mr Roberts was always telling me I needed watching if anything was to be got done. And here was Mrs Roberts giving me the whole enterprise as casually as you might hand over a sweetie to a child. 'Thank you,' I said, trying to inject as much fervour as I could in my voice so she'd know what it meant to me. 'You won't regret this, I promise. I'll never let you down.'

Mrs Roberts put her hand on my arm to stop my gushing and held out the key to the till. 'I will come back at the end of the day to sort out the takings,' she said. 'You are a good girl, Molly. We have been lucky to find you, Mr Roberts and I.'

After she'd gone, I went back to bed to think. I knew I wouldn't be able to sleep because I was too excited to even close my eyes. Yet another new life was suddenly clicking into place. I was going to become a surrogate daughter to Mr and Mrs Roberts, who would both die soon and leave me the stationery shop in their will. This would be the perfect front for my work as Tim's assistant. I would recreate Miranda's room up here, turning the rest of the floor into a luxury bathroom and kitchen, where I'd prepare tasteful but healthy meals for Tim. We'd be the beautiful and mysterious couple everyone envied. I clutched the key in my hand. I wasn't going to let it go.

I was just redesigning the shop layout in my mind so that I could sell books as well, a little corner with an armchair people could feel comfortable in, a coffee machine next to a plate of homemade cakes, when I heard a banging on the door downstairs. I looked at my clock and realised it was a full half hour after opening time. I threw on my clothes, ran my fingers through my hair and rushed downstairs. Then I had to run upstairs to find the key to the till.

Apart from the bad start, the rest of the morning went so well I shut the shop at twelve and gave myself an hour off. I felt ready for anything, even Charlie Canterbury. I stood in front of the mirror, breathing myself into my alias and then I ran to the library, keeping close to the buildings as I'd seen Tim doing, ducking into alleyways when I could. I didn't make eye contact once, although I was hoping the passers-by were all looking at me, envying my sense of purpose, my directness.

But then I saw Joe from school again. I thought of calling out but it was only his back view retreating, and I'd didn't really want him to see me anyway. He must have had another dentist's appointment.

As I watched him, someone bumped into me and I cursed loudly. To my amazement they said sorry so I did it again, just to make sure. And then every time I knocked into anyone in that busy street, I just huffed and they apologised to me. Normally it worked the other way round. You obviously didn't mess with Charlie Canterbury.

Liz was standing at the back of the children's section, her arms crossed tightly in front of her. I followed her gaze and saw a man in his twenties sitting on one of the giant ladybird floor cushions. He was working his way through a stack of picture books.

'Trouble?' I asked quietly as I sidled up next to her.

She gave a start. 'I didn't see you there, Molly,' she said. And I smiled with pleasure. I'd be better than Tim at the secret agent thing at this rate. We'd be the beautiful, mysterious *and* invisible couple. 'It's just Malcolm,' Liz continued. 'He comes here every week and always gets the same books out to look at. I was just wondering if I couldn't get him to have a go at something more challenging.'

I looked at Malcolm. He was opening flaps and pulling paper levers with evident enjoyment, taking his time on each page before turning to the next.

'He looks happy enough,' I said, but Liz wasn't convinced.

'I don't mean he has to read Dostoevsky,' she said, 'but I think he might be able to cope with some kind of story at least.'

As we watched, Malcolm started to pick his nose thoroughly, wiping his fingers on the cushion. I put my hand over my mouth in disgust, but Liz just sighed and picked up the pile of books that were on the shelf behind her. 'There's almost too many,' she said. 'I never thought I'd say this, but I'm not sure we couldn't get rid of half the books in here. I see people come into the library full of good resolutions, but after five minutes browsing the shelves they lose their will to live, let alone read. They slink out empty handed and go home to watch the television instead.'

'I didn't,' I said, trying not to look at what Malcolm was doing now. 'But then I suppose you helped me choose.'

I followed Liz through to the adult fiction section. 'How's Bob?' I asked. 'I think you're such a perfect couple together.'

She slammed books hard from one side of the desk to the other. 'Married,' she said. 'And not to me.'

I muttered something about being sorry.

'It's just all so sordid and predictable,' she said. 'I didn't even have to ask him. I had all the information at my fingertips. I looked him up on the library files and there it was. The whole history. His wife has a penchant for trashy thrillers, although I did notice she's started to take out large-print books. No wonder she doesn't realise what's going on in front of her eyes.'

'So you're not seeing him any more?'

'Of course, I am,' she said. 'But the prospect of a pension added that extra something.'

'Maybe you're his still true love though,' I said.

She sorted her way firmly and with precision through the piles of books sitting in front of the computer. 'Maybe, but why should I be the one who does all the work while Mrs Romantic Thriller scoops the final rewards?' she asked.

I stayed silent because I couldn't think of anything to say that wouldn't annoy her. I'd seen how white her knuckles were as she clutched the date stamp. Charlie Canterbury could probably have given advice on poison or general first-wife murdering skills but she must have left the library when Liz and I were concentrating on watching Malcolm.

'Anyway, enough of me,' she said eventually. 'How are things going with you?'

I grinned. 'Brilliant,' I said. 'I can't quite believe it all.' I wanted to tell her about Mrs Roberts and the shop, but now didn't seem to be the right time.

Liz smiled. 'You've blossomed, Molly. It's been a joy to watch. So you really want me to choose you a book?'

I nodded. 'Although—'

'Had enough of romance?'

'No! I wondered about something actually written in French. Do you have those?' I asked.

'Have we done Nin?' she asked. 'Not traditionally French, of course, but I think she'll pass.' And then she went off to search the foreign language shelves before handing me the thinnest book I'd had from her yet.

When I got back to the stationery shop, the closed sign was still up but the door was unlocked. I pushed it open gently, trying to think of excuses for why I'd shut up shop in case Mrs Roberts had come in while I was at the library, but no one was there. There was no sign that anyone had come or gone.

My hands were shaking as I checked the till. All the cash from this morning seemed to be there. I walked round the displays. I couldn't see any obvious gaps or damage.

'Hello,' I called out, my voice quivering. No reply. I went upstairs to check, but everything was just as I left it. I must have left the door unlocked myself. I bustled around, putting on the kettle and making some tea to take back to the front of the shop, but I still couldn't get rid of a feeling of unease.

Luckily the shop was busy that afternoon. In between customers,

I rushed round clearing up displays, making sure nothing was out of place, taking pleasure from flicking open the blank pages of the notebooks, even colour co-ordinating the box files so they created a rainbow on the shelf. I wanted Mrs Roberts to be *enchantée* with me. She didn't have to know I'd left the shop open to all comers.

She came back at six. I quickly hid my French novel. Of course, I hadn't understood any of it, but it had given me tingly feelings just mouthing the words out loud. 'Bonjour,' I said brightly to Mrs Roberts. 'S'il vous plait?'

'Hello Molly,' she said, peering round the shop. *Ello.* I almost tasted the accent. *Ee-lllloo.*

I proudly handed her a sheaf of handwritten A4 sheets.

'And these are?' The eyebrow she was raising was just one hair thick. I tried not to see how it gave her the look of one of Miranda's porcelain dolls.

'I thought that rather than just rely on the till's takings, I'd write out each transaction in full today. That way you can double-check against stock and money. Make sure I'm doing the right thing.'

I expected her to be pleased. The whole procedure had taken much longer than I expected and had held up the customers so much that one had left without buying anything, but it was what the assistant did at the card shop down the road and I wanted to prove I was just as trustworthy as him. He ran the shop for weeks on end sometimes.

Mrs Roberts ran her finger down the figures. 'Very satisfactory,' she said, before screwing the pages into a ball and aiming them neatly in the bin. I held back a gasp. 'No point giving yourself extra work though, is there, Molly? I always say actionwork is better than paperwork. And Mr Roberts will continue to be absent tomorrow. You will carry on coping so well, yes?'

My disappointment quickly turned to pleasure as she praised me. I straightened my shoulders to mirror her perfect posture. 'No problem,' I said. 'I just hope he gets better.'

'And you, Molly, you will be going out tonight, I think? Somewhere young and romantic?'

Rrrromaantick. I thought of Tim. We were planning to practise setting and breaking codes together in the park tonight. I nodded. 'We'll probably go to the pub,' I said.

She smiled as if this was the right answer, and then slipped the cash from the till into a cloth bag and drew her jacket into her chest, before taking a quick look round the shop.

'The box files look good,' she said as she was leaving, proving Mr Roberts was right. She saw everything.

'There's a lot I can do here.' I walked to the door with her. I didn't want her to go. 'I've got ideas.'

She paused in the doorway, her painted nails tapping on the woodwork. 'I have been thinking that maybe on Sunday, you and I could go through the whole shop,' she said. 'Reorganise everything. Mr Roberts is a man. He doesn't understand the importance of detail. But you, I think that you know this. Would you like to work with me like this?'

I nodded and she rested her hand on my hair briefly. 'You would look very chic with a chignon,' she said. 'Maybe you will let me show you how to do it the proper way. The French way.'

I put on Miranda's dress and went round to see her. She was sweeping up the bits of loose hair left on the floor. The dustpan was a nest of different colours.

'Mrs Roberts is putting me properly in charge,' I shouted above the music she was playing. It hadn't been Bryan Ferry for a long time. This was some guitar music it was impossible to sing along to. 'She's letting me help her do up the shop and everything.'

'Nothing I wouldn't expect,' she said, brushing the hair into the bin. 'Aren't I always telling you how clever you are?'

'You are,' I laughed. I danced round the shop, holding my arms out and twirling.

'Careful!' Miranda shouted. I stopped dead, surprised. She was watching me, her arms crossed in front of her, a half smile on her face. 'So I suppose you'll be wanting a new hairstyle now you're boss, will you?'

'Mrs Roberts is going to teach me how to do a chignon,' I said. 'It's a French hairdo.'

'I know.' Miranda stopped smiling and turned her back on me, clearing up the towels although they were already in perfect order. 'I *am* a hairdresser, after all. Although not French, that is true. Boring old English Miranda, that's me. But there's some that thinks that's good enough. Customers who come back month after month and don't complain.'

'I didn't mean anything. It just came out wrong.' And just as quickly as that, I felt hopeless and deflated. I hated Miranda for spoiling everything.

She must have sensed my change in mood. 'I'm sorry,' she said. 'I've just got things on my mind. I can do you a chignon if that's what you want. It might not be perfect but I'll do my poor old best.'

'It'll be perfect. Thank you.'

Something had changed between Miranda and me. For some reason the image of Joe's perfect white teeth flashed into my mind.

'The dress looks nice,' she said. 'You've certainly got the wear out of it. I've got more stuff at home you can have. I'll bring it over to you one day and you can try it on.'

'I could come to you.' I was turning my head from side to side in the mirror. 'Miranda,' I asked, 'is it just me or is my face looking thin?'

She put her head down to my level. 'I was wondering that myself, Molly. Are you sure you're OK? You have registered with a doctor and everything here, haven't you?'

'Of course,' I lied.

'That's fine then.' She carried on doing my hair in silence for a few minutes, but then I couldn't hold it back any longer.

'Miranda, why do you never talk to me any more?' I said. 'You're the only one I've ever really spoken to about my father, but you've never asked me anything else.'

'If you want to, you'll tell me.' She stood back to admire her work. My hair was scraped back all the way round my face, with two little tendrils curling down at the sides. It was pretty, but it wasn't perfect. Not in the way I knew Mrs Roberts would do it. 'Do you want to tell me?' Miranda asked.

'No,' I lied. How could I talk to her when her face was tensed up like that? 'There's nothing to say. But thanks for the hairdo.'

'You've lovely hair,' Miranda said.

'So who am I like?' I prompted her, but she looked blank.

'Remember that thing we used to do when we first met? "If your hair was a film star, it would be a blonde Elizabeth Taylor."'

'She had black curly hair. Yours is still gingery from when you got me to dye it, Molly.'

I sighed. 'Never mind.'

'You must come for your tea again soon,' Miranda said. 'Mum was asking.'

'Was she?' I tried not to seem too keen.

'So what are you doing tonight?' Miranda said. 'Going out with your famous Tim to celebrate?'

'He's busy. You don't fancy doing something, do you? A film or even a drink in the pub.'

Miranda laughed. 'You and your pubs. No, I'm meeting someone. Another time, Molly.'

She opened the door for me then and I stood there, unsure whether to give her one of our old pecks or not. 'Go on with you, silly,' she said suddenly, pulling me to her and giving me a big hug.

I waved goodbye to her from the street. I could see her through the shop window, but she didn't seem to notice me. She stood in the middle with her arms out and twirled, just as I had done, but she wasn't telling herself to stop. She's happy, I thought. What's Miranda got to be so happy about?

THIRTY-FIVE

I went looking for new clothes armed with a list of instructions Mrs Roberts had given me and the two extra twenty pound notes she'd taken from the till and passed to me as if it was a secret we were sharing. She'd tut-tutted the first time I told her that was how Mr Roberts had paid me, insisting instead that things should be done properly. Now, she left me thirty pounds in a sealed envelope by the till every Friday. 'The pocket money,' she called it. 'After all, you are a lucky girl to have your lodgings here.'

She still hadn't come upstairs to see my room and I didn't want to tell her that her 'pocket money' was considerably less than the amount Mr Roberts ended up giving me when he wanted extra time up the ladder. I told myself I could just keep cutting down on food.

New clothes were different though. Mrs Roberts was prepared to open the till for that so I could dress more how she imagined a shop assistant to look. I kept getting out her list and reading it, although I knew it by heart by now.

Point number one: Buy the most expensive you can afford. I went to the charity shop further up the High Street and started flicking through the rails. There was only one other person in the shop with me, a smartly dressed businesswoman who must have brought in the two black sacks the shop assistant was sifting through. 'Oh thank you,' the shop assistant kept saying as she pulled out yet another black skirt. 'These are just lovely.'

I pulled out a green pleated skirt and held it up against me in the mirror. *Point number two: Think of the ideal picture of yourself. Does the garment match this?* I put the skirt back and took out a red sequinned mini dress instead.

Point number three: Amusing things can be fun, but are always add-ons. It is more important to get your basic framework right. There was a black waistcoat on the headless dummy that caught my eye. Worn over the top of Miranda's dress, I could see the ideal picture of myself as someone fragile and yet individual. 'Could I try that on?' I asked.

The shop assistant, all tight curls and tight lips, kept sighing as she made a big fuss of taking it off the shop model and handing it to me. 'You do realise it's for a man, don't you?' she asked in a loud voice that made the businesswoman giggle. I didn't have to look up to picture the raised eyebrows.

'Of course,' I lied. I would have bought it now even if I hated it, which I didn't. An idea was forming in my mind.

Point number four: Always, always check seams. They are an important sign of how well made the garment is. I checked the waistcoat seams. No fraying. They'd even been double-turned. Inspired now, I left the women's section and started rummaging through the men's and then the boys'.

Point number five: Individual style is exactly that. Individual. I took armfuls of clothes back to the mirror.

Point number six: Think of the whole. However beautiful a garment is, if it doesn't match with anything else in your wardrobe, you won't wear it. 'I'll have all these,' I said, taking a pile over to the counter. She smiled at me then, but I didn't smile back. 'And some of those ties.' I pointed to the heap of silk ties that must have just come in and hadn't been sorted yet. 'The brightest coloured ones you can find.' They would look good against some of the T-shirts I'd chosen or as make-shift belts, but what

I really wanted was for her to have to get on to her knees and grovel before me. I was the customer after all. It was a heady feeling.

THIRTY-SIX

'Turn your head to one side. Gently. Not as if you're on a military parade. Now try walking again, the way I showed you before.'

I made my way from the back of the shop to the front, thrusting my left shoulder forward to match my right hip, and then the opposite with the next step.

'Right shoulder, left hip,' Mrs Roberts was almost barking at me from behind the till. 'How hard can this be, *Mollee*? Come on, try it again.'

I shuffled to the back of the shop.

'Bright smile,' ordered Mrs Roberts. 'Remember appearance is everything. Now, left, right, shoulder, hip. That's right! You are looking like a lady, a proper French lady.'

I looked up at her with excitement and tripped over my feet, knocking into the envelope display. 'Back to the beginning, Molly,' she said. 'Once you've got this, we'll try it with a book on your head. Get the angle of your chin just right.'

We were so busy, neither of us noticed Mr Roberts come in. He stood hunched in the doorway, smiling at both of us.

'There you are, chéri,' she said, when she eventually saw him. 'And what do you think of my transformation?'

I slumped in front of him, embarrassed, but Mrs Roberts clicked her fingers at me. Quickly I pushed my hips forward so my torso was straight, one leg in front of the other, the heel of the front foot slightly raised.

'The shop looks very nice,' Mr Roberts said, ignoring me.

I guffawed, but Mrs Roberts looked annoyed.

'I meant Mollee, Juelles.' She pointed an elegant finger at me.

'Oh, she's looking lovely, dear.' But Mr Roberts was staring at his wife, not me. 'Very neat and proper. You're working magic as usual.'

Mrs Roberts clicked her fingers at me again. 'You can relax now,' she said. 'I have to go out for a bit before we go home, Jules. You will be fine, yes?' She picked up her bag and gloves, and then with an air kiss waved towards both of us, she was gone. The door shutting behind her like the final click of her fingers.

'It's nice to have you back.' I fussed about, getting us some tea and telling him about the customers, until I realised it was true. In a funny way, it *was* nice to have Mr Roberts back. There was something comforting about the way he pottered around, checking everything. He had a new stick he leant on heavily, pausing only to tut-tut about all the changes in the shop until I told him they were Mrs Roberts's idea. Then he walked round again, his head to one side as if he needed to look at it all again from a different angle.

'What a woman,' he wheezed, as he walked back to the counter. I pushed his mug of tea over to him. No white china for Mr Roberts. 'I bet she's teaching you a thing or two, isn't she, Molly? Although, you must admit, it'll take a lot of work to get you under control.' He laughed as if this was a joke we should both be sharing.

I put my hand up to my hair. Miranda didn't work Mondays so at least she wouldn't spot the perfect chignon Mrs Roberts had done for me. My shoulders straightened automatically, my chin at the right level for eye contact.

'So how's the boyfriend?' he asked.

'Busy,' I said. 'He's involved with this big project at the moment which is taking up lots of his time, but it's not something I can really talk about.'

'Sounds important.'

I nodded.

'It's just that Mrs Roberts has been worrying about you,' he said. 'She said something about a note she'd found. Sometimes she gets a little, ah, French. Not that she's not perfect, but they can be more emotional at times.'

The *Help Me* note. I could have kicked myself. I'd forgotten about that night. In fact, I hadn't even thought about Leanne for days.

'Mrs Roberts hasn't said anything to me,' I said.

'You know her. She's not one to get involved, but she did wonder if you had everything you needed.'

'I'm happy,' I said, and the strange thing was that it was true. I felt fulfilled. My life had taken off in new ways I would never have expected a year ago. Every day was like a holiday. For the first time ever, I went to bed longing to wake up so I could enjoy the next day. But I still wished she'd talked to me herself.

'You are a funny girl,' Mr Roberts said but he was looking at me fondly. Not in the way he usually did when he said things like that about me. 'And you like Mrs Roberts?'

'Oh yes.' I cursed the enthusiasm in my voice when I saw the look he gave me.

'The thing is, Molly,' he said, 'I'm still a bit poorly, so I'm not going to be able to come into the shop so much any more, and Mrs Roberts and I wondered how you would feel about working with her more or less full time. She's been a wonder about it all. It's not really her thing, of course.'

'That would be fine.' This time I was tactful enough not to seem too keen. 'I'll miss you, of course.'

He nodded, liking this more. 'We've got on all right, haven't we?' he said.

'We have,' I agreed.

'Told each other some rum little stories.'

'We have.'

'You've done me proud, you know. I spotted something in you when I saw you outside the Church, but I never expected you to turn out such a nice girl. Just proves . . .' He fell silent.

'Proves what?' I asked.

'You shouldn't judge on first appearances.' He wheezed his way into a full scale cough. I could feel my eyes narrow and my heart start to race as I waited until he was finished. 'You must admit you were a bit rough,' he said, eventually. 'Wondered what I was letting myself in for.'

I was surprised to feel the old fury fill me. It had been so long since it last came that I had hoped getting angry was just a stage I'd been going through, as the counsellor had said. But here it was coursing back through my body like an old enemy that just wouldn't give up. I felt cold with what . . .? Rage, fury, pique, outrage, resentment that other people were always going to be telling me I was something I knew I wasn't, and the way I always believed them. I tried to do the breathing exercises the counsellor had taught me, but instead I mumbled something towards Mr Roberts. I was longing for him to get out of my shop now with his coughing and ill old man smells and to leave it to me and Mrs Roberts to clear up nicely.

'What's that?' He was still beaming, congratulating himself on dragging me out of the slums.

'I was never rough,' I said.

He let out a sudden roar of laughter. 'You were like something the cat dragged in,' he said. 'A big fat lump, sitting there weeping and putting the fear of God into everyone.'

And then, all of a sudden, something strange happened. The monster rage that had been threatening to ice me over unexpect-edly melted. This wasn't something that had ever happened before.

It normally built up instead, starting with something trivial and ended up with me freezing off any emotional response to the person or situation so I wouldn't have to feel any more. And that's when I needed to do the pinching, or worse, just so I'd know I was still alive. But now the thawing was physical. I relaxed down from the top of my head, my stomach settling as the tension left, and then I started laughing too.

'I did scare that Church woman,' I admitted.

It seemed like such a long time ago. A different Molly. Now, I needed to keep my energy for the bigger picture. With Tim, I was part of something important.

There was a toot on the car horn from outside then and Mr Roberts and I shook hands formally as he left. I handed him my hand the French way, loose at the wrist and light at the fingers. I stood up straight as I saw that Mrs Roberts was sitting in the car, adjusting her hair in the mirror as she waited for him.

'But you'll come back to the shop sometimes?' I asked. I was shocked by how thin his fingers were, and the way his frail wrist stuck out from his cuff like a stick I'd easily be able to break in two. When I stood this close to him, I could see the skeletal outline of his skull. He even stumbled slightly as I let go of his arm.

'Mustn't keep her waiting,' he said, 'but Molly?'

'Yes?'

'Keep Leanne safe for me. Promise?'

I agreed, even though I wasn't quite sure what it was I was promising.

THIRTY-SEVEN

With Tim's memory training, I had to look at something, in this case a patch of grass, and then shut my eyes and list as many things as I could about it for five minutes.

Grass is grass though. I got up and walked over instead to the tree opposite. Although the leaves were starting to fall, several of the branches were bowing under the weight of new pictures and messages that were tied on them now. I undid two hearts and took them back to the bench to read.

I wish for peace, not war.

The writing on the first heart was childish and scrawling. The heart had been cut out with blunt scissors which meant straight edges and paper tears. A snail's trail of glitter glue brightened up the cardboard. Four sequins had been stuck on at random but when I flicked one with my finger, it fell off and lay on the path, glinting in the sun.

I turned to the second heart. It was beautiful. Whoever had made it had woven different coloured ribbons in and out through the card, and created a collage of those see-through sweet wrappings so it looked like stained glass. A white label was stuck in the middle.

BE SAFE.

I turned it over. That was all. *BE SAFE.* No name. No other message. Tim came up then so I handed it to him.

'That's nice,' he said, crumpling it up and dropping it on the ground. He hugged me to him so tightly his belt buckle was pushing into my skin.

'Good news, Charlie,' he said. 'Everyone's really pleased with the preparation we're doing on the mission. I think that we'll be ready to go very soon. How does that make you feel?'

'Excited?' I asked hesitantly. I wasn't sure what was the right answer. It might have helped if I had some idea what I was letting myself in for, but I still hadn't confessed to Tim how I'd slept through my briefing.

He tried to lift me up playfully then, but I was heavier than he thought so he stumbled. 'Careful,' I said, but he wouldn't leave it alone. He picked me from just below my bum, hoisting me over his shoulder.

'Tim,' I cried, 'put me down.'

'You're my spy,' he shouted, half-running along with me across the path by the side of the playground. 'My beautiful mission partner. My secret adviser. My very own Charlie Canterbury.'

A teenage boy walking a dog stopped and stared at us. 'Crazy people,' he called out, but in a friendly way. Tim waved at him. 'I love this woman,' he yelled, and as we passed I could see the boy wave back.

'I'm too heavy for you,' I shouted.

'As light as a feather,' he said, although when he finally put me down with some relief I could see the sweat drops forming on his hairline. I put my finger up and wiped them off his skin, and then put it to his mouth. He licked the tip of my finger like a cat. 'So, spy,' he said.

'Yes, spy,' I replied.

We both smiled at each other.

'I thought we weren't supposed to draw attention to ourselves,' I teased.

'I forgot myself,' he said.

I felt warm inside. 'How do you fancy a treat?' I said. 'I've got an idea.'

We walked hand-in-hand, but just as we were approaching the pub, Tim stopped. 'No, Charlie. You're right and I was wrong. It's not safe for us to be seen together like this. Not so near to the start of the mission.'

'You're not the only one with a plan,' I said. I pulled him to the side of the pub and into the dark empty beer garden. 'Listen.' I put my ear to the wall. Reluctantly Tim came to join me.

I'd found that the bricks had a different feel here than other places I'd tried: the department store, several houses, even Miranda's salon when she wasn't looking. I was learning to pick up the different vibrations in the foundations. I knew Tim would be proud of me.

'Can you hear?'

Tim nodded. 'Are you getting what I'm getting?'

I put my ear closer. All I could make out was laughter and confessions and jokes and in the background, a life story droning on and on.

'This could be important,' Tim said. 'Good work, Charlie.' He pulled out a small notebook from his back pocket and started making some notes.

'What can you hear?' I asked. I was resting both palms against the wall now, feeling the warmth from the building settle into my skin.

'I'll tell you later,' Tim said. 'When it's safe.'

'Do you know what I'd really like to do?' I asked Tim.

'Anything,' he said.

'Stay out all night and watch the stars.'

We went back to the bench and Tim put his coat round both of us. 'Are you cold?' he whispered.

'Yes,' I said, letting my body fold into his as he held his arms tighter around me.

When you looked up at the whole sky you could only see a few stars at first. They seemed to twinkle and disappear. But if you forced yourself to focus on just one bit of the sky, then stars that had been invisible started to come forward and make themselves seen. More and more until what had previously been just a blank bit of black turned into a sparkling fairyland.

'It's just like life,' I whispered to Tim, 'you have to really look because you don't always see everything the first time.' But he had slumped forward over me, his turn to fall fast asleep. 'Some spy,' I smiled, determined to watch out for both of us from now on.

I was practising Mrs Roberts's walk – right shoulder, left hip – on my way through to the shower room at the gym when I caught sight of myself in the full length mirror. I stopped dead. And then, looking round to make sure there was no one else there, I opened the towel I'd draped round me. I put my hips back, my left leg forward, heel up, and stared at my naked body for a few seconds, before covering myself up quickly.

Even in the shower, as I was standing shivering under the icy cold water, I was thinking about my reflection. I was like something from a magazine. I was picture perfect. As thin as a model. You could have hung clothes on my hipbones, kept jewels between my neck bones, hooked cups on the nobbles of my spine.

I was lean, mean, dangerous. I loved myself.

THIRTY-EIGHT

I was finding it hard to keep any control over Liz and Bob's affair.

Some days I'd go into the library and she'd be bubbly and excited. But other times, I'd have to look away from her so as not to let her see I'd noticed her red, swollen eyes. 'Love hurts,' I'd say then. 'If it wasn't painful, it wouldn't mean anything. I bet he's feeling worse, at least you can take consolation from that.' Her book reading swerved from one of Bob's interests to the next, as if she was on some manic coach tour, always one country behind.

One evening, I came to the library just before closing time to find her reading the history of the island of Corsica, because that was where he was taking his wife for an early winter break.

'You could get away too,' I suggested. 'Go somewhere romantic. Do it properly.'

'Who with?' she said, and then before I could answer: 'And what with? I'm not made of cash. Unlike someone and his large-type wife. Anyway, I'm fine.'

Every morning for the last two weeks, Liz had gone out and bought a copy of the *Daily Telegraph* with her own money so Bob wouldn't have to keep up with the news on the hated computer. She kept it, pristine clean, under the desk so if he came in, she could surprise him with it. More often than not, she'd had to throw it away unread at the end of the day.

Even I could see it wasn't going well.

'I wonder if you aren't making it too easy for him,' I said. Liz had

189

just received an inter-library loan of a book about Westminster School, where he had apparently spent the happiest days of his life. She had it in front of her on the desk as we spoke, fiddling with the cover. 'He fell in love with you when you weren't very nice to him, after all.'

Liz stopped stroking the book and looked up.

'Maybe you just need a strategy for love, or something.'

She shrugged her shoulders, but I could see she was still listening.

'Make a plan. Play a bit hard to get. Act a bit cool.'

'And how do I do that?' She seemed to be asking me this seriously.

I shut my eyes. Willed all my French ladies to totter into my mind on their stiletto heels, with their razor-sharp silhouettes and even sharper tongues. I let all the words I'd read over the last six months swill around my head for a few minutes and then I opened my mouth to see what had stuck enough to come out.

'Sometimes what you have to do is to imagine what people think about you, and enter that reality for a moment,' I said. 'In your case you have to create a different reality for him.'

Liz was nodding, so I continued. 'You've got to make him think there's someone else in the picture, but not just anyone. Imagine everything the accountant has ever wanted from you and dangle that in front of him so that he can see what's on offer from you, and what he's in danger of losing.' I was in my flow now, remembering all the women I'd read about and the efforts they went to to make their lovers jealous. 'What you need is a hotel room, with white sheets and big windows. Somehow you need to make him think you're going to this hotel with another man, let him picture all the things you're getting up to in there. Perhaps he could even burst in, find it empty but there's a red silk negligee draped on the enormous double bed which is drenched in your perfume.'

For a moment the only thing I could think about was how proud my father would have been of me now if he could see me giving useful advice. And not just to anyone, but to a librarian no less.

As I left the library, I was swinging my bag of books by my side, when I saw Joe again. I was sure this time despite the short, yuppy haircut even Miranda would approve of, but when I called out his name, he nipped into a side alley and by the time I reached there, it was empty. Pity, I thought, running my tongue over my teeth. His parents must be spending a fortune on his orthodontics.

By the time I got back to the shop, I was still thinking of different ways Liz could seduce the accountant, so I didn't notice that the door was unlocked again until I was inside. Even then it was only when I automatically put up my hand to the light switch that I remembered I'd deliberately left the lights on when I left. Someone had been in and turned them off. I stalled my hand, and peered into the gloom of the seemingly empty shop.

It would have been sensible then to run outside for some support but something made me go on. I went back to the door and kept my hand clutched on the handle as if that would make it easier to get out in case of trouble.

'Mrs Roberts?' I called. 'Is that you?'

No reply, but then there was a sudden crashing noise from upstairs.

The street had been half-deserted as I walked here. That twilight time between the shops shutting and the bars getting busy. The only people I'd seen were the two bouncers from the basement club, chatting to each other as they stood guard. I was trying to think how long it would take me to call out to them for help, when there was another loud banging. It sounded like heavy boxes being thrown around the room.

Mrs Roberts wasn't strong enough for that kind of work. Besides it would ruin her nails.

My heart was punching up through my head and right into my ears now. I ran frantically, moth-like, to the door that led up to the stairs, and then to the window, and back to the rear of the shop. I was looking for someone to help me, for somewhere to hide, for a weapon to defend myself with. Anything. Truth was I didn't have a clue where I was going, what I was looking for. I hiked Miranda's dress up around my waist so I could move quicker. I wished I was wearing something more protective. An invisible cloak would have been good. Outside, a car drove very slowly down the street, illuminating the window display briefly in its lights, but it was gone before I could think about calling for help.

And then seconds later, the shop door opened from the outside. I squinted but I couldn't see anything clearer than two dim shapes through the dark glass. The door opened wider until a triangle of street light appeared on the floor. I squatted down by the envelopes, curling myself into the wall, ignoring the pain of the shelf edges as they dug into my body.

'Tim,' one of the shapes called out, and it was only then as I sighed with relief that I realised I'd been holding my breath. I started to uncurl myself, to stand up straight, when the lights in the shop snapped on. I paused, blinking, before crouching back down to watch what was going to happen. Just in case. A middle-aged man and woman were standing in the doorway. The woman stared around the shop hopelessly, but the man carried on shouting. 'Come now, Tim. It's all right. We're here.'

I pulled Miranda's dress down to cover my ankles, smoothing my hands over the material as much to comfort myself as anything. Apart from that, I stayed still. The banging upstairs stopped then.

We were all paused, like characters on freeze-frame. I kept my eyes on the door leading up to my room.

'Tim,' the man called again. 'We know you're here.'

He moved further into the shop, as I shrunk back into the shadows. If it was Tim upstairs, he'd know what to do. I didn't want to spoil anything.

The man called up the stairs. Then silence again, broken only by the sound of someone walking downstairs, one slow step at a time.

'Thank God.' The woman rushed forward and hugged Tim as he appeared. He looked thin and small and tired. It was hard to imagine this was the same person who'd sat on my bed just the night before, raking his hands through his hair with excitement as he outlined more of his plans – big plans – for our future.

'Get your stuff together,' the man said. 'We're going to take care of you. You'll be OK now.'

Tim stood completely still. Tell them, I prayed. Tell them that you're with me now. That we're looking after each other. Tell them that you can't leave me.

'Let's just go,' the woman said. 'This place gives me the creeps. We can come back later, Timmy, if you need anything from here, or get you everything new. That might be the best thing.'

Tim didn't look up from the floor. If he had, he might have seen me. And then would things have been different?

The woman had her arm around him now, and it was clear she wasn't going to let go as she led him out of the shop. It was only when the man bustled after them that I remembered how to move. I ran out, and watched them get in the red estate car that was double parked outside.

It worried me that the car made no noise as it drove away, but I could see the back of Tim's head through the rear window. He looked like a child being taken on a treat. I willed him to turn round and say something to me, but he didn't. I was left waving on my own. I kept my hand up for some time after the car had gone, imagining the sad picture I made, the perfect French tilt of my chin. It was only after I'd gone back inside, I realised Tim hadn't looked out for me once. He hadn't said a word.

I locked the door and went upstairs. There I pinched myself hard. Shut my eyes and kept on pinching until a wall of pain wrapped round me like a comfort blanket.

The park at night became my sanctuary. There was a time between eight and ten o'clock when I could pretend it was nearly all mine. The kids who would normally be there kicking a football around or practising on their skateboards had long gone home, and the late-night gangs of teenagers and kissing couples hadn't come out of the pubs yet.

A few dog walkers were doing their rounds on the outside paths. I liked to imagine them going home and talking about me; the mysterious girl who sat alone on the bench. 'She was there again tonight,' I could almost hear them calling out as they shook the night off their coats at the door before moving into the warmth and the light.

I shifted along the bench to make a space for where Tim would normally sit, and then I started to cry. This was a regular thing now. I allowed myself twenty minutes exactly, weeping with my head between my knees, and then I'd shake myself, wipe my face with one of the two spotted handkerchiefs I'd bought from an old fashioned man's shop I'd started going to for accessories – Mrs Roberts had stressed how important these were – and walk back.

One day though, about three weeks after Tim left, I caught sight of something from my upside down position. I tried to focus through my tears and reached down to pick up the walnut from the ground. I finished crying five minutes earlier than usual, rolling the nut round and round between my hands so I could feel its roughness against my palms.

It hadn't been there before. I could swear it. Which meant someone must have put it there. I walked over to the tree and placed it carefully in a fork of the branches where it wouldn't fall, pressing it safe with my index finger. I pulled off three hearts from around it so they wouldn't knock it down, crumpling them up and throwing them in the bin. I didn't feel guilty, there would be more tomorrow.

THIRTY-NINE

'How's Mr Roberts?' I asked Mrs Roberts as she fussed over the window display I'd just spent several hours arranging.

'He is fine,' she said, moving a pile of gaudy notebooks from one side of the desk to the other and then back to where I'd originally put them.

'Is he ever going to come back?' I was just standing with my arms crossed and watching her although I knew it would get me into trouble. I should at least have some files in my hands so I could pretend to be busy, but I couldn't be bothered.

'Probably not.' Mrs Roberts stood up and rubbed her lower back. She was dressed head to foot in beige. Even her perfectly waved hair seemed more wool-like and knitted into shape than my jumper. I ran my hand through my hair.

'Ah Molly.' She leant over and smoothed it down immediately. 'A French woman would never let herself get messy like this. And so thin. Believe it or not, there is such a thing as too thin.'

I knew my style was getting more 'individual' than she would have liked, but I was now just as obsessive as her about getting things right. It took a lot of time to dress how I did. The truth was my new look felt Charlie Canterbury-ish, and I was learning to take comfort in that because it was all I had left of Tim.

I knew I was dressing like a boy, although Mrs Roberts kept insisting I was going for the urchin look. As I found it harder and harder to eat every day, I had to agree she was right about me getting too thin. I'd rest my hands on my hipbones sometimes when I stood still, feel them move under my palms as I walked upstairs.

'I'd like to see him,' I persisted. 'Could I come and visit one day?'

'And why would you want to spend time with an old man?' Mrs Roberts asked, looking up only briefly from the felt pens she was now testing. 'When I was your age, I was out dancing with boys my own age every night. A young girl like you, with the world at your feet.'

I looked down at my shoes; white basketball trainers with yellow and white striped laces. 'I'm not like you though,' I said, realising as I spoke that it didn't make me feel as sad as it might once have done.

'That, darling, is quite clear.' And she laughed, brushing imaginary dust off the shoulders of my waistcoat, and pulling straight the tails of the man's white shirt I was wearing. She clapped her hands, just touching the ends of her fingers together so the acrylic sheen of her false beige nails glittered under the bright window lights. 'And now back to work, Molly. So much to be done.'

Always so much to be done. These days there was rarely any time to think, but I wasn't sure the shop was any busier than when Mr Roberts was running it. I climbed the ladder and pretended to be sorting out the boxes on the top shelves, although in reality I was just watching the dust motes and counting the threads on the spiders' webs.

'Molly, would you make tea?' she called up about fifteen minutes later.

While the kettle boiled, I laid the white cotton napkin on the tray and placed the flowered bone-thin china cup and saucer carefully on top. I couldn't resist tapping the silver spoon against the china as I rested it in the saucer, but the milk I poured without

spilling a drop into the small jug. Teapot warmed, I made the tea
and brought it through to Mrs Roberts at the counter.

'This is good, Molly,' she said. 'Not just this, but everything here
today. Well done. You're not having yours with me?'

'I'll take it in the kitchen,' I said. 'Just have a bit of a breather.
It's hard work up there.'

I sat at the table and inhaled the steam from my mug. It was
too quiet nowadays. From the shop, I could hear Mrs Roberts
humming to herself as she went through the files of paperwork
she always seemed to have around her.

'I really would like to see Mr Roberts please,' I said, going through
and standing in front of her. 'Just to chat.'

'If you wish, Molly.' She looked up and frowned at me. 'But he
doesn't live at home any more.'

'Not with you? Where is he then?'

'Where they can take proper care of him. He is happy there, I
think.'

'He can't be. He'll miss you terribly. Oh, I must see him.'

Mrs Roberts leant over and pushed my hair back behind my ears.
'Your hair, Molly. You must keep it neater. Go and sort yourself out
in the mirror.'

Right shoulder, left hip, head straight, chin up, neck like a swan,
appearances being everything, I bit my tongue and sashayed off
to the toilet.

I went over to the salon to find Miranda. 'I want you to cut my hair.'

'Have you never heard of the word please?'

'Please will you cut my hair?' I tried again.

'No.' She turned back to her magazine.

'Miranda,' I complained, suddenly unable to stop myself. 'You
never have any time for me these days. I know you don't want to
talk to me, but you used to beg to do my hair. Can't we get back

to how we were? Why does everything have to change? Is it me? Have I done something wrong?' I was horrified to feel the tears come.

Miranda quietly passed me a tissue. 'Sit yourself down, girl. In fact, there's a style I was looking at just here that would be darling for you.'

I looked. The model had long, ironed hair cut along the bottom with a zigzag edge and a fringe coming below her eyes. 'Are you serious?'

Miranda gave a peal of laughter. 'Not on your nelly.' She clapped her hands together. 'But at least it made you smile. So how do you want it?'

'You're happy,' I said, remembering seeing her dancing round the last time. 'And you're too busy to see me. I think I know why.'

I was putting two and two together and making one. Joeand Miranda. Of course. Every time I'd seen him, he'd been around the High Street but not at the dentist. Instead, he'd been coming to see Miranda. It made perfect sense. She had been watching me that day and had asked about him. He must have come back and she met him then. That's why she'd been cool with me. I didn't know what lies Joe had been telling her. Or even what he knew.

Miranda started combing my hair out. 'I want it short,' I said. 'Really short. You know, like a skinhead.'

'Are you sure?'

I put my hand out and felt the wall of the salon. Only good things happened in here. 'Yes,' I said. 'I'm going to see Mr Roberts tomorrow. I'd like to give him a surprise.'

Miranda smiled at me. Not the old girly grin but a real smirk that made me smirk back. 'Let's go for it,' she said. 'But I'm not shaving it off.'

She took a long time shampooing and washing my hair. 'This could be the last time I get to wash your beautiful long hair,' she said as she checked the temperature of the water against her arm. 'So are you going anywhere nice on holiday this year?' She put on a sing-song voice.

'Paris,' I said. 'In between New York and Morocco. One finds one needs the sun at this time of year.'

'Lovely.' Miranda pulled my wet hair up above my head as if she was measuring it. 'So why am I so happy then, clever Miss Molly?'

'A man.'

'Wrong.'

'I am so not wrong.'

'Couldn't be further from the truth,' Miranda crowed.

We moved over to the chair, my hair wrapped up in a towel turban. 'I'd shut my eyes for the next bit if I were you,' Miranda said. 'I'll tell you when it's too late to turn back and then it'll be safe to open them.'

She pottered round for a moment and came back with some scissors and a handful of pins.

'Put Bryan Ferry on,' I begged. 'Just for me. Please.'

'I'm not sure we've still got it, but I'll look.'

She went over to the music system, hunting through the pile of CDs and soon our favourite old ballads started to fill the salon. I felt myself purring. 'Some customers are easily satisfied,' she said. 'So any man, or did you have a particular one in mind?'

I looked strange with my hair looped up on one side. Miranda took her scissors and cut about four inches off at once. I gasped. 'Told you to keep your eyes shut,' she said. 'Listen to the music instead. Doesn't that always tell it as it is?'

The way you look tonight . . . We both smiled.

'I think it's Joe,' I said, blowing away a strand of cut hair that landed near my mouth. I could hear Miranda's intake of breath and her sudden stop of motion.

'Joe! Are you for real? He's about six.' She was squealing.

'He's almost the same age as us, older than me,' I pointed out. 'But you have met him, haven't you? You've been seeing him? Otherwise how would you know who I mean?' Above me, my eyes now shut, I could hear Miranda bustle back into action.

'OK, I'll be honest. He did help me with college applications, that's all. Although, when I first asked him, I think he agreed because he thought I was doing it on your behalf but he was still as nice as pie when he realised it was really was for me. Very fond of you. He said you were the pin-up at school.'

'Joe's helping you go to college?'

'Just the forms. I couldn't think who else to ask.'

'But how did you meet him in the first place?'

'He popped into the salon about a week after he bumped into you, wondering if anyone knew you. Apparently you'd promised to go for a drink with him.'

'I did not,' I said.

'Anyway,' Miranda ignored me, 'we got talking and he was telling me all about how he was going to university.'

I could just imagine that.

'And I suddenly got all Gloria-like and thought it should have been me.' She sang a few words and then laughed to herself. 'I should have gone straight from school like everyone said.' I could feel her letting the pins on the other side down now. When I put my hand up to feel my neck, she pushed it away. 'Better not, doll. Not just yet,' she said.

'Why didn't you go?'

'Life.'

'No, what happened really?'

'Life's not enough for you any more?' There was a catch in Miranda's voice as she tried to make a joke of it and failed. I guessed she was staring at herself in the mirror because she stopped cutting momentarily. 'No, there was a teacher at school who used to encourage me a lot. We liked the same kind of books. Had some of the same silly dreams even. I suppose he saw me as a kind of project, and we became friends. But all sorts of people got the wrong end of the stick and the headmaster called him in one day and threatened him with I don't know what, and he left the school just like that. Without even saying goodbye. I felt so sick about it all, I just gave up too. I'd been working here as a Saturday girl so as soon as I could I came here to work full-time. It hasn't been bad but, I don't know, after getting to know you and everything, I started to want more.'

'Me?'

'Can I tell you the truth without you getting upset, Molly?' Miranda's hand was flat on my head now, holding it straight. I could hear her heavy breathing as she concentrated hard. I kept my eyes tight shut. If there was one thing I didn't want to hear it was the truth, but Miranda's voice kept coming. 'I didn't want to end up like an older version of you,' she said. 'Content to waste all your potential. That was one of the reasons I let Joe talk to me about you at the beginning. I suppose I wanted to understand what happened to you so I'd know something about myself too.'

'I'm not stuck.' I was suddenly reminded of how Liz once told me I'd never be nothing.

'No, of course. You've got spy-boy, haven't you?'

'Tim,' I corrected her automatically. I hadn't told Miranda, hadn't told anyone about the night Tim left. I tried to change the subject. 'So what did Joe say about me?'

'Very little actually. It seems you were as much of an enigma then as you are now. One minute you were the most popular girl at school, the next you were a recluse and then the next you were gone. Apparently they still talk about you, but no one can find out anything. I think Joe was hoping I'd give him some clues.'

'Did he talk about Leanne?'

'He asked if I knew someone of that name. Said she'd gone to France or something. Who's she then?'

'A French girl. She went home,' I said.

'And what about the elusive Molly then? Are you going to tell me?'

I opened my eyes then to look at her, but at that moment caught sight of my own reflection instead. 'Oh holy fuck.'

'You like it.' It wasn't a question. Miranda leant back, scissors in hand and smiled at me through the mirror.

I ruffled the short layers on top, rubbed my fingertips over the graduated stubble at the back of my neck, pulled the two side bits down until they made kiss curls on my cheeks.

'I love it.' And the best thing was that it wasn't Molly looking back at me at all. It was Charlie Canterbury. We winked at each other. The potential in the mirror was almost frightening.

'Do you want to tell me about how you came here?' Miranda repeated. 'Now I've told you about my English teacher, you'll know why I'm not a great one for sharing secrets, but I'd like to know yours.'

'You've never asked,' I said.

'I am now.' She leant over and forked gel through my hair with her fingers, getting the hair to stand up at the front. Charlie Canterbury looked back at me from the mirror, her lips were tight-shut.

'Too late.' But I stood up and did a very un-Charlie like thing then. I kissed Miranda on the cheek. 'Thank you,' I whispered. 'You really are the best.'

FORTY

Summerfields had the wrong name. It should have been called Wintergraveyard. This was clear even before I'd gone through the depressingly smeared and dirty glass doors. The red brick one-storey building enclosed a concrete courtyard, round which was hung a collection of hanging baskets filled with what looked like dead twigs. There were mounds of mouldy leaves blocking the two drain holes; the three wooden benches were dripping with bird shit, one was missing a plank at the back; and in the middle of the courtyard there was something that resembled an old boot.

I squinted to see it better. It was an old boot, left to rot on its side. The smell of weak wet cabbage mixed with disinfectant got stronger as I waited in the reception area for someone to answer the bell I'd just rung. I tried to calm my nerves by reading the line of framed certificates hanging crookedly from the flocked wallpaper. At least the staff were properly trained, I thought, until I realised that they all belonged to the same person. Dawn Carey.

It wasn't a surprise, then, when the person who bobbed up behind reception was wearing a white apron with Dawn embroidered on the front pocket. She reminded me of a hedgehog, all squinty eyes and dark hair sticking up like prickles. When she beamed at me as if we were old friends, I found myself smiling back.

'They're all in the sitting room,' she said. 'It's time for the music and movement class, my favourite.' Sure enough, I could hear a piano from down the corridor, thin voices singing out an approximate rhythm. 'Although I can't say that to our other volunteers,' Dawn giggled. 'I tell them all that they're my favourites, even the sugared flower petal lady, and we all fall asleep in that one.'

I nodded. 'I'm here to see Mr Roberts,' I said.

Dawn clapped her hands. 'A visitor,' she said. 'How wonderful. Why don't you come and join the end of the class? There's only another quarter of an hour to go. It would be a shame to miss it.'

'I'll wait,' I said.

Dawn looked so disappointed it was all I could do to stop myself changing my mind. She tapped her fingers on the top of the desk and kept looking down the corridor.

'Please don't let me hold you up,' I said. 'I'll be fine on my own.'

'Well, if you don't mind,' she said. Everything about her was scrubbed and clean, but in a good way. Mrs Roberts would love her. I wondered if I'd like working here as much. I could imagine the two of us together like a pair of angels, cheering up the old people's lives, doing good just by our presence. What would my favourite activity at the home be? Somehow I didn't think it would be music and movement. I'd probably like the sugared flower petal class. Dawn and I would have little rivalries about it, egged on by the happy patients.

'Does Mr Roberts enjoy music and movement too?' I asked her quickly, before she left.

Dawn smiled at this idea. 'He hates it.' She leant over the reception as if she was confiding something. 'We made him go for three sessions because his wife insisted, but now we just let him stay in his bedroom and pretend to her that he's attending. Naughty, but we thought, well, that maybe the French men she was used to were different. To be honest not many of our men here are the dancing kind.'

I stared at her. 'So he's not in there,' I asked.

'Oh no, he's in his room,' she said. I began to wonder if she wasn't so much enthusiastic as simple-minded.

'So can I go there and see him?'

'Of course. We're not a prison here.' But she'd skipped off back down the corridor before she could tell me where his room was.

I'd almost given up on finding the room when I opened Mr Roberts's door. I thought he was asleep at first. It was the first bedroom in the whole corridor I'd looked into which had someone in it, so I peered at the lump on the bed for a bit. Then I recognised the tweed jacket hung up over the chair. The smell of tobacco and overripe fruit.

I half-shut the door again and knocked lightly.

'Come in.' His voice was weak and small. I paused for a minute before I walked in.

'Molly?' Mr Roberts sat up. He was wearing blue and black tartan pyjamas, the top unbuttoned so his pale chest was showing. 'Molly girl, is that you? What the heck are you doing here?'

'Mrs Roberts sent me,' I said.

He was searching on his bedside table for his glasses. 'Let me look at you,' he laughed. 'Well, aren't you a sight for sore eyes?'

I did a mock curtsey. I'd rolled my trousers up to mid-calf, so that my yellow tights showed over plimsolls I'd painted green. My new short hair was tucked under a black beret. I pulled it off to show him though and put my head down so he could ruffle it.

'Well, I wonder what Mrs Roberts has to say about your new look,' he laughed. 'She's quite something, isn't she?'

I tried to smile. 'Something special. Mr Roberts, are you terribly ill?'

'I'm being well looked after,' he wheezed. 'Can't complain.'

'But you're not that old,' I said. 'You shouldn't be here.'

He looked down. His hands were spread out over the sheet and

I could see how thin his fingers were. His skin was almost papery white, like something we'd sell in the shop.

'It's for the best,' he said. 'Mrs Roberts and I agreed on it.'

'Mrs Roberts lets me run the shop sometimes now,' I said.

'Does she? I bet she's got it all going like clockwork.'

'We miss you though,' I said. 'I . . . I wondered if you wanted a story.'

He smiled. 'That would be grand, Molly. For old time's sake.' And when I sat on the bed, he put his hand out to hold mine.

'I used to do this with my dad,' I said. 'He'd make me tell him how much I loved him.'

'No Leanne today, I suppose,' Mr Roberts said and I shook my head. He sighed, shutting his eyes.

'Although this story really is because of her,' I said. 'Remember how I told you how she used to steal things and give them to me.'

Mr Roberts's head moved slightly. I took it as a yes.

'Well, I used to keep them in my bedside drawer. I'd take them out sometimes, line them up on my bed and look at them. There was a lipstick, a small sequinned purse, two thin silver bangles, a book of poems, an enamel fish key ring, a hand mirror with one of those proper handles, a pretty cigarette lighter, some perfume. Nothing very big, but there was a lot of stuff there.

'And then, of course, one evening my father walked in without knocking. He saw everything there and he didn't say a word. He didn't even ask if any of it was mine; he just swept it off my bed with his fist and stormed out. I could hear him shouting at my mother about how I'd been stealing. That she was to take me into school the next day and make me confess to the teachers.

'He was screaming that I was no good, that he was fed up with me, that I didn't have any hope for the future. I could hear Mum just agreeing with him. That's what hurt most.

'He came back later that night and took all my clothes, apart from the nightdress I'd been wearing. He said he wanted to make sure I didn't do anything stupid. I wrapped the blanket round and round myself but I still couldn't get to sleep.'

'You went out though in your nightdress, didn't you?' Mr Roberts looked as if he was speaking from a coffin, but he still remembered everything I'd told him, and not just about Leanne. I stroked his hand to let him know I was grateful.

'Not that night,' I said. 'Anyway the next morning, I persuaded Mum not to come in with me to see the teachers. She's not a strong woman so I knew I'd get my own way. She kept saying that Dad would kill her and that I must promise to only tell the truth. I will, I said. Your father, she said. My father, I replied. That was enough for both of us.

'Anyway, I went straight to the biology teacher and said I had something to tell her. "Can't it wait?" she asked. She was one of those fluttery sorts. Lots of scarves and always late for everything.

'"No," I said, "but I can come back this afternoon when you're less busy."

'So that afternoon, I told her what I'd been planning since the night before. I said that I couldn't stand it any longer. That was all I meant to say but my stories went on and on, getting bigger and bigger, wilder and wilder. I was almost scared of myself. I told her that my father had been doing things to me that weren't right.

'I still don't think I wanted her to actually do anything though. Just telling someone these things was revenge enough. I walked out of that biology classroom feeling fuller somehow, even though I'd just emptied myself of all that poison. To tell you the truth, I couldn't even remember what I'd said.

'But the biology teacher remembered every word. A social worker called Jane came to the house that night to take me to a hostel. My mother refused to come with me, but both she and my father turned up the next morning. I wouldn't have anything to do with either of them. My father was white with fury. I could see his hands ball up into fists as I stood at the top of the stairs, watching them.

'"See." I pointed his hands out to the social worker. "I'm scared."

'I couldn't stop crying. If things had been bad before, it was like I'd stepped into a nightmare now. They took me back to the bedroom and told me I wouldn't have to worry any more. The next visit I had was from my mother on her own. She said I wouldn't have to see my father any more.

'I asked if he'd gone to prison but she shook her head. "Never mind about him. It's just you and me now, sweetheart," she said. My mother had never called me sweetheart before. I took it as a good sign.

'We went to stay with Mum's sister in Doncaster that week for a little holiday but ended up staying nearly two years. Mum didn't call me sweetheart again. We never even discussed Dad, but I'd catch her looking at me sometimes, just after I came out of a bath, or when I was watching TV in my pyjamas and I'd see the same hatred I saw from my father's eyes. She was judging me. Wondering if I was turning out as bad as he thought I would. I suppose she thought she might not be able to manage me by herself.

'No one ever had any great hopes for me at school. To be honest, I never really went if I could help it. By then I was too busy eating. I couldn't stop. It was like I wanted to anchor myself on solid ground. To protect myself in a cloak of fat. And then one day, I just took some money from my mother's purse, told her I was going out to the pub with some friends, got on a train and ended up here.

'And then I found you.' The tears were streaming down my face, but when I looked up, Mr Roberts was fast asleep.

FORTY-ONE

I couldn't sleep that night, so I was awake when I heard a loud banging on the shop door. I tried to ignore it, so frightened that I almost persuaded myself that the noise was the commotion from my agitated heart, but when it went on I crept downstairs to see what was happening. Tim was standing under the street light. I ran over to hold the door open wide.

'Come in,' I gestured.

'No!' He looked up and down the street like a bad actor.

'You're being followed,' I said happily. 'Is it time for us to get going at last?' I licked my palms quickly and flattened my hair down in the mirror. Charlie Canterbury getting ready for action.

'Worse than that,' he said. 'I have arranged to do what they say, but they will not win. Here.'

He thrust an old black canvas shopping bag into my hands.

'Take this and guard it with your life,' he said.

I nodded and he looked at me gravely, as if he were taking an impression of my face to remember me by.

'Come in.' I was suddenly frightened, as if I did think there was someone out to get him. 'I've missed you so much.'

'Goodbye, my love.' He was already down the street, striding out resolutely. I watched him turn the corner before I shut the door.

When I opened the bag, I wasn't surprised to find a jumble of old newspapers. But there was something else as well. A grassy, wet earth smell I remembered from childhood. I scrabbled in the bottom of the bag and pulled out a bundle of white fur. The puppy was so small it fitted on to my palm, shivering and making a little mewing noise. Tim must have taken it away from its mother, it could only have been about a few weeks old. I prayed this was the only one he'd taken.

'Shhh . . .' I whispered to it, trying to dredge up a lullaby or something I could sing, to soothe myself as much as the puppy. Unable to think of anything else to do, I took the puppy to bed and went straight to sleep, deeper than I had in weeks. I woke late to delicate little licks and a wet patch in my bed.

To my surprise, Mrs Roberts fell in love with Mata immediately.

She brought in a padded velvet dog cushion for her to sleep on in a quiet corner of the shop, a small porcelain water bowl which she filled with tea at our break times, a thin pink collar with gold heart studs all the way round which she fixed on as carefully as a lover giving a diamond necklace.

'It's my birthday.' Mrs Roberts came into the shop one morning with three strawberry tarts in a white bakery box, tied up with a red ribbon.

'Three?' I asked. I had a sudden hope Mr Roberts might have made a miraculous recovery and be coming to the party. I hadn't been back to see him since my last visit, and when Mrs Roberts never mentioned it, I decided to take it as a sign that I'd had a lucky escape this time round from the danger telling my story could bring.

'Well, one for Mata,' she laughed. 'Did you think I would leave her out?'

I danced around the birthday girl, sitting Mrs Roberts down on the one good chair, fetching her a cup of tea to eat with her cake, a nice plate, even a fork. She nodded as she inspected the tray. I laid it like clockwork these days. 'An extra plate for Mata, I think,' she said. I went through to the kitchen to fetch one. There, I had to hold on to the counter for a second. At times when I was least expecting it, the pain from not seeing Tim hit me with unbearable force. Sometimes I could just about manage to split myself off and carry on almost as normal, but at others, such as here now, there was nowhere to turn.

'Mollee,' Mrs Roberts called. 'Are you all right in there?'

I splashed my face with cold water from the sink and came out chin up, smiling with Mata's plate. 'You spoil her,' I said, as Mrs Roberts fed Mata a dollop of cream from her own fork. Mata's little pink tongue lapped greedily.

Mrs Roberts smiled. 'This is very nice, Molly,' she said. 'And what about Mata's papa? Have you heard from him?'

I shook my head. I'd told everyone that Tim was away on business. Important business, I'd added. He'd got a friend to give me the dog.

'Well, he must love you very much if he leaves you such a beautiful pet to keep you company,' she said.

'Did you have lovely birthdays when you were a child?' I asked, changing the subject. 'In France.'

And probably because she saw the tears welling up in my eyes, she told me at last about her childhood, how poor it was, how a fear of poverty kept her awake at night. 'Do you know one year I got a potato for my birthday?' she sighed. 'My mother had drawn eyes and a nose and a mouth on it, sewn a little sack dress for it, but it was still a potato. And I had to pretend to be happy.'

'I bet you kept it thought,' I said. There was something sweetly familiar about Mrs Roberts and her potato pet. Leanne, I suddenly clicked. It was exactly the kind of thing Leanne would have done. No wonder Mr Roberts liked hearing about her.

'We ate it for dinner.' To my surprise Mrs Roberts clapped her hands together and laughed. 'Look at your face, Molly. That's why I've never had children. I might cook them.'

I tried to smile along with her, but I was shocked and it was hard to hide it.

'Oh you are so young. I forget you have such little sophistication.' I'd disappointed her again, but it was so easy to do. She had such high standards. I couldn't imagine how she put up with Mr Roberts and all his habits. Maybe that was why he needed me. We all need someone we can feel superior to.

'Mr Roberts saved me from all that poverty. I owe him my life.' It was as if she was reading my thoughts. 'And the idea of going back makes my blood chill.' She shuddered at the thought.

I nodded. Mr Roberts was quite a regular up on his white charger saving young women. I wondered what conditions he had imposed on Mrs Roberts. There are, after all, always conditions.

'What's wrong with him?' I asked. 'He will get better, won't he?'

Mrs Roberts dabbed at the sides of her mouth with her white napkin. 'No, Molly. It's his heart. He's very weak. One shock and that will be it.' She drew one perfectly manicured finger across her neck. 'There's no point being sentimental. You English cry too easily over dogs and old men, and always when it's too late. More important to keep him alive as long as we can, and then when it's time. Well, it's time.'

'You won't miss him?'

'I will cry. But on the inside only. It's important to keep the face on, no? This is something I think you're learning fast.'

It soon turned into a competition between Miranda and Mrs Roberts over who could love Mata the most.

'You honey-bunny,' Miranda said the first time she came into the shop and saw Mata lying in state on Mrs Roberts's cushion.

She crouched down, knees creaking, to get on to Mata's level. 'You little bunchy-munchy. I could eat you all up, oh yes I could. You're like Shirley Temple, you are. I'm going to put ribbons in your curls, and take you out to tea.'

'Give over, Miranda,' I said. 'She's blushing.'

'Are you turning reddy-red then?' Miranda did a bouncy thing with her head, and I was pleased to see Mata look to the side as if in disgust. 'Pinky-winky, doggy-dog. Oh, she's a poppet. Bring her home. Let Mum see her.'

'I'd like that.'

'Oh you,' Miranda cooed at Mata. 'You're coming to Miranda-wanda's homey-womey to see my mummy-yummy.' Mata put her tongue out to lick Miranda's cheek and Miranda squealed. 'Do you love me?' she said. 'Do you love your Miranda then?'

Mrs Roberts and I both stood with our arms folded, watching Miranda as she eventually stood up. 'It's almost as if she can understand,' Miranda beamed. 'I'm sure she smiled at me then.'

'If she could understand, that dog would do the vomit right here and now,' Mrs Roberts whispered to me. 'You have to keep your dignity with animals. Otherwise they have no respect for you. Animals and men, both the same.'

'And before it's too late,' I said, just so she'd know I'd been listening to her lessons properly.

She escaped to the kitchen then to have a few minutes quiet. She'd looked pointedly at Miranda when she announced this, leaving the two of us alone.

'She hates me,' Miranda said.

'No, she doesn't,' I lied. 'It's just that she's more reserved than other people. She's been through a lot.' It wasn't that I was giving any of Mrs Roberts's secrets away, just hinting that I knew a lot more than I was letting on.

'I suppose so,' Miranda looked doubtful. 'And all these financial worries can't help too.'

'What worries?'

'Oh you,' Miranda sighed rather than cooed. 'You've your head in the clouds. This shop isn't exactly a hive of activity, is it? The big shops in town are clearing up nowadays. People want more choice.' She gestured round the half-empty shelves. 'And all Mr Roberts's medical care will be costing a pretty penny too. My boss reckons she'll only last a few more months before she'll have to sell up.'

I hadn't thought about any of this before, but now I remembered coming back from a walk with Mata just earlier that week and noticing Mrs Roberts through the shop window. She was sitting at the cash till, reading a letter. I watched her rub her forehead again and again, before she pulled out a perfectly ironed white lace handkerchief and started mopping her eyes.

I'd turned and pulled Mata after me. I just thought Mrs Roberts looked as if she needed some time on her own. I imagined her reading an old love letter from Mr Roberts. By the time I got back, she had her face on and I'd forgotten about it until now.

'She'd have said if there were serious problems,' I pointed out to Miranda.

'Would she? She doesn't give much away, does she? You're two of a kind. Regular mystery women. Made for each other.'

'If she sells the shop, I lose my home,' I said. I could feel myself icing up inside.

'Oh ducks. It won't come to that. Besides, it's hardly the Hilton here, after all.'

I ignored this. 'And there's Mata now too,' I said.

'Oh, you can come and live with me,' Miranda dived down to rub noses with Mata. 'Can't you, doggy-dog? We'll be happy-wappy, cosy-dosy.' Miranda stood up and saw my face.

'What about me?' I asked.

'You're not really worried are you? Couldn't you go and stay with your parents until you find somewhere else?'

'No.'

'I'm sure it will turn out for the best,' Miranda didn't sound convinced. 'Och, don't you fret, I wouldn't see you out on the streets. And especially not Mata, would I, lovely-dovey?' And Mata rolled over and exposed her stomach, as Miranda started petting her all over again.

FORTY-TWO

I went to the park and sat on the Seize the Day bench. My head was hurting. A dark-haired man stopped to pat Mata, but I just yanked on her lead and he walked off. I rested my face in my palms and rocked backwards and forwards. I could think of nowhere to go, no one to help. It was as if a chasm had opened and swallowed up everything good.

There must be something I could do.

Without hope, I went to stand outside the pub and rested my open palms on the rough bricks. Nothing. I even put my ear hard against the wall. My head was completely empty.

All I had to look forward to was silence.

And what made it worse was that because I'd told no one that Tim had gone, there was no one to tell that I *had* seen him recently. Just the once.

On the evening of Mrs Roberts's birthday, Mata had been restless and yappy. I put it down to too much cake and tried to ignore it, but eventually I gave in, pulled on my coat and went downstairs to talk her for a walk.

There was a note slipped under the door of the shop. It must have been what was troubling Mata.

Meet me in the pub at seven-thirty, Tim.

Tim was back and he wanted to meet me. Not even at the bench. No, he was going to take me for a drink at the pub. A proper drink in a proper pub. This was what I'd dreamt of. At last I was going

219

to be normal. At seven-thirty. I looked at the shop clock. I had twenty minutes to get ready.

I ran back upstairs, sat on the edge of my bed and tried to breathe. On the wall above my bed, a series of pencilled gates marked off the days since I'd last seen Tim. I counted them. Twenty-two.

I stood up and went over to the mirror, ruffling my hair so it looked even more boyish. My eyes seemed huge. Mrs Roberts had shown me how to put on black eyeliner and to brush rouge not just on the apple of the cheek but in a sweep across the cheek-bone and up to the sides of the face. I'd stolen some of her make-up, some French cosmetic brand in heavy gold packaging I'd never be able to afford on my own and I guessed she wouldn't miss. She had even plucked my eyebrows one day when the shop was quiet.

I wondered if Tim would recognise me. I could creep up behind him in the pub without him noticing, show him how much work I'd been doing on the programme he taught me, impress him enough so that when he went away next time, he'd take me with him. Charlie Canterbury, special agent.

Oh Tim, my special adviser.

My only.

You.

The shortest love poem in the English language.

You.

I'd paused for a moment outside the pub, trying to breathe normally. I could hear the laughter from inside, the snatches of conversation, lines of pop songs from the juke box. I stood to one side to let a man go in front of me. As he entered, a gust of warm air came back outside to hit me. I could have stood there for ever.

Once inside I spotted Tim immediately. He was sitting in the corner, wearing a heavy black overcoat I hadn't seen before. His hair was unbrushed and he was staring into an empty pint glass in front of him. When I came over, he shifted up to make room on the bench next to him.

'This is nice,' I said and he nodded.

'Can I get you a drink?' he asked after a few seconds of silence. I asked for a tomato juice, but when it came I wasn't sure what to do with the plastic stick that came in the glass. Every time I took a sip, it pierced my cheek. Eventually I took it out and put it in the ashtray. Tim watched all this with a grave slow interest.

'So,' I said, 'how have you been?' I was determined not to ask him anything about the mission or his advising. Let him come to me. Let him tell me everything. With animals and men, it is important to retain your dignity. That way they respect you.

The pub was more folksy than I had imagined from the outside. It dripped with authentic-looking photographs of village cricket teams and old music-hall posters you know have been bought from some out-of-town warehouse. The rest of the customers looked as if they'd been bought by the yard too; their golfing jumpers and silk scarves fitted in so well with the non-threatening atmosphere. I huddled with Tim in the corner, half afraid the other drinkers would be angry if they noticed how much we spoilt the picture.

'Miranda's well,' I said. 'She goes to college one day a week now. She comes here, I think, with some of her new friends.' She'd told me this casually, obviously forgetting how often I'd begged her to come with me and she'd always refused.

'And Mrs Roberts has got the shop shipshape.' I started to laugh. 'The shipshape shop,' I explained when Tim looked puzzled. 'It's almost a poem.'

Tim fiddled with the beer mat, shredding the edge with his thumbnail. I picked up the swizzle stick and tapped it a few times against the ashtray. What did we used to talk about? Maybe normal was overrated.

'When the kids at school used to go to the pub at lunchtimes,' I said, 'they'd always come back talking and laughing, smelling of smoke and alcohol. The teachers would turn a blind eye. They said it was just part of daily rebellion.'

But I wasn't in the mood for storytelling tonight and Tim didn't seem to be listening. I sipped my juice and looked round.

Suddenly he spoke. 'I've been having badminton lessons,' he said.

I snorted into my drink so violently that the juice came out of my nose. It was a strange feeling as if my nostrils were fizzing. I roared with laughter, clapping Tim on the back, looking round proudly because I thought at last he'd proved himself to be stronger, more exciting, than the rest of them. But he wasn't smiling. In his hands, he held the pub menu advertising Christmas meal specials.

'Perhaps we could have a game sometime,' he said, and he looked, his face puffy and square, like someone I'd never met before.

Keep your face on. Don't let anyone know what's going on in the inside. Tim kissed me on the cheek when it was time to go, and I walked away from him across the park, head and chin up. I didn't look at the Seize the Day bench and I definitely didn't turn round to see if he was watching me to make sure I was safe.

FORTY-THREE

Liz was the only one not joining the Mata fan club.

'You can't bring it in here,' she said, tapping the No Dogs sign on the door as she shepherded me out of the library quickly.

'She's a her, not an it,' I protested.

'No difference. Still no dogs. Tie her up if you want, although she'll be safe. No one would take a mongrel like that.'

'But it's cold. She'll freeze.'

'It's the rules,' Liz said, rubbing her hands together to warm them up. 'Now, are you going to come in or not? I've got the kettle on.'

When Liz bustled around like this, I knew things weren't going well with the accountant. As we walked through the library to her office, she stopped to yank a book away from a toddler who'd been left in the children's section while his mother hovered round the romance paperbacks, picking herself out some of what Liz usually called paper Valium.

'He was eating it,' Liz told the woman defensively as the child started screaming. 'Please don't bring your kids into the library if you're not going to look after them properly. We are not a crèche.'

'So what's happened?' I asked when we were sitting down having our tea. I'd quickly put aside all hope of Liz being sympathetic about Mrs Roberts's predicament today.

Liz spent some time straightening everything on the desk, making sure that the ruler was aligned perfectly with the pencil sharpener. 'I told him I was going away for the weekend,' she said eventually. 'I even booked myself into the hotel, left out the card on the desk here' – she pointed to a spot on the surface – 'so he could see it, acted all mysteriously and a little bit sexily.'

I looked at Liz's tightly curled hair and tightly buttoned-up cardigan. For the first time, I noticed that the lines at the side of her mouth were drooping downwards, giving her the look of one of those puppets with hinges on their jaw. She twiddled with the string on her glasses.

'Sexy, that's good,' I was as enthusiastic as I could be.

'Well,' she banged her tea mug down on the desk and then had to get some tissues to mop up the spill. 'I went, and only spent the whole bloody weekend on my own. Even if I wanted to leave the hotel I couldn't because I'd only brought a certain type of clothing with me. They'd have thought I was some kind of tart, in town to pick up business.'

I tried not to look too startled at the thought of Liz as a travelling tart.

'And it cost me a fortune, what with the single supplement and all that room service. Money which, I don't need to remind you, would be better off put to my retirement fund.'

'Did he say why he didn't come?' I asked. 'Maybe something terrible had happened.'

Liz spoke icily. 'He decided to take advantage of me being away by treating his wife to a night out. He said she deserved to be spoilt for once. Apparently, they both enjoyed it enormously.'

This wasn't going well. I racked my brains for something useful to say. 'Still, in the long term it shows you have another life,' I said, throwing back words I'd picked up from Mrs Roberts. 'Appearances are vital; you can never be sure when you're being looked at. Even small gestures could build up the bigger picture.'

Although Liz was staring at me, her hands were still busy

tidying up the immaculate surface of her desk. Her fingers traced the perfect edge on the pile of books in front of her.

I carried on, hoping something I said would stick. It was harder work than I thought. 'Maybe he's only pretending not to mind. He could be tossing and turning now thinking over exactly how you spent the time away. He may even be ringing up the hotel now, asking for the exact same room you had so he can visualise the scene.'

'He's playing golf with two retired solicitor friends this afternoon,' Liz interrupted. 'And he knows just how I spent the weekend. I told him.'

'Oh, Liz, you shouldn't have done that. It spoils the mystery.'

Liz looked at me as if mystery wasn't something, after all, she could quite see. Then she did something surprising. She leant forward in her seat and put her face in her hands, rubbing her eyes against her palms. I felt oddly let down. But then she raised her head, and I saw her eyes weren't ringed romantically with tears. They were sharp and glittering, but more with steel than water.

'Did you deliberately set out to hurt me, Molly?'

I was silent, sitting on my hands, only half wanting her to stop talking. I had the strangest feeling that at last I was going to find out some truth about myself that I needed to know.

'Look at me, Molly,' she said, lifting up my chin so I was staring into her eyes. I saw they were finally filling with tears. 'I'm fifty-two, not seventeen. I'm flesh and blood. I need three tablets before I can even think about functioning properly every day. Nothing romantic about that. Do you know how I felt in that hotel room, all on my own, with a whole wardrobe of inappropriate nightgowns?'

I shook my head again.

Liz was pulling out tissues from the box and mopping her face before dropping them on the floor and picking a new one. She wasn't a clean crier, someone who would dab at their eye with a lacy handkerchief, like Mrs Roberts. Or even an efficient one, like me in the park. Her tears were black with streaky mascara, running down her face to join the snot from her nose. I had no idea what to do, so I got up and ineffectually patted her back.

'Go home, Molly,' she said. 'I've nothing left for you. I'm all out of stories.'

I clutched at her hand to make her feel better and also because I wanted her to engulf my smaller hand in hers again. Mother and daughter, I thought. She's going to look after me. Everything's going to be all right.

'Just leave me, Molly,' she whispered, taking her hand away.

'None of this was you,' I whispered then. 'You don't have to pretend it was you suggesting things to me. I did it on my own. You were my story.'

'Get some help,' she said. 'For all our sakes.'

'Shall I come back tomorrow?' I asked. 'When you're feeling better.'

'Leave,' she repeated.

I picked up Mata and we started to walk quickly home. I felt strangely excited, but wasn't sure if this was the right emotion for the occasion. I tried several others – anger with Liz, boredom at yet another adult telling me I'd got things wrong – but the tingles in my stomach kept bringing me back to excitement.

Just as we were getting near the High Street, I veered off left and decided to go looking for Tim instead. We'd go to the pub and I'd take him up on that badminton game, I thought. I'd show Liz that it could be done. Tim and I could buy a house together, or maybe just a flat to start with. I'd look after him. We'd live happily ever after. I persuaded myself that Mata could sense if he was near so when she got a scent of something and her tail started to wag, I rushed after her, letting her go where

226

she wanted until, finally, she stopped at a discarded bundle of fish and chips.

I wouldn't let her smell them, pulling her away roughly as a punishment. It was in my knees I felt the disappointment most. I was so scared they were going to buckle under me. I rushed over to the wall to hold me up and it was then I saw him.

I'd learnt from Tim to keep my gaze down on the pavement and never, ever to look into people's faces, but for some reason, I couldn't stop looking at the tall, thin man getting out of his car. It wasn't Tim. I didn't think it was for a moment but still something made me move my eyes away from his brown shoes and up to his face.

'Are you all right?' he asked and I nodded. He looked me up and down for a few seconds before turning to go through the black door of his house, shutting it firmly behind him.

I watched the door for a few minutes, and then one of the windows where I could swear I saw a curtain twitch. I memorised the door number, the street name, the colour of the woodwork, and then I pulled Mata along the street after me, my face hot. I went into the public toilet and stood in front of the mirror, fingering my hair until I looked less like a boy and more chic. Almost French.

When I came out again, I could see men everywhere I looked. It was as if I had woken up, had the scales ripped from my eyes. A wave went through my whole body, breaking in the pit of my stomach and sending me spiralling down the street. I had to hold my legs together in case this feeling gushed out of me and drowned the passers-by. And what passers-by they were. So many men. My head felt as if it was being controlled by a puppeteer, it was swinging from side to side to get a better look.

Mata and I stayed out for hours and hours after that, just walking and looking.

FORTY-FOUR

By the time we got back, Mrs Roberts had closed up for the day. She'd left a note for me taped to the till.

Where have you been? We'll speak tomorrow. A man came to see you. He said he was your father.

I crumpled it up and chucked it in the bin.

My father.

I was numb. I walked round the empty shop, my arms stretched out so my fingers could touch the goods. I pinged a nail against dangling sales notices so they trembled in front of me; I stuck my hand in the still fan imagining the carnage if I turned it on by accident; I opened scissors, holding the blade against my wrists and pushing down so the skin tightened; I put my tongue against the serrated edge of the Sellotape dispensers; my forehead against the cash drawer of the till and opened it again and again so it hit my eyes each time. Surely there must be a way I could get myself to feel something?

And then when I was bored with all this, I picked up the buff file Mrs Roberts had been looking at that time I'd watched her through the window. She must have left it behind. It was full of typed letters. I read the top letter once, and once again. I skim-read the second letter, and third, and fourth. Banks, accountants, estate agents. Pleas for more time, more money. All initialled with the loopy signature Mrs Roberts once told me all good French girls learnt at school.

I took the whole file up to my room. Mata followed me, pausing before she jumped up each step as if it was a mountain she was being forced to scale. Her tail was wagging with excitement, her head tilted to one side as she took each jump and I thought, not for the first time, that there must have been some reason why Tim had given her to me other than the fact she was someone to love and who would love me.

Mr Roberts wouldn't let Mrs Roberts sell the shop. She'd written that to the bank: 'My husband is convinced this is a temporary economic downturn.' This was next to the letter from the lawyer about how she wasn't to worry about the medical bills because they were being paid for against the sum she would inherit after Mr Roberts's death. What the letter didn't say was that, without the medical bills, the amount was big enough to solve all her current problems and save the shop. But I could see that.

Look after Leanne. I bet Mr Roberts had no idea about what was going on. Protecting him from worry was Mrs Roberts's way of showing gratitude for all he'd done for her.

I went upstairs and found my mother's book, counting out about half the money and putting it in my pocket. There was something else to do before I took my next step, someone else to rescue.

Mummy was kissing Santa Claus through the department store's sound system as I walked in the doors. 'Seems to come so quickly these days,' a customer complained to me as we passed on the escalators. I couldn't agree, the kiss was taking such a long time that Mummy was still busy by the time I reached the third floor, and hadn't even unglued those lips when the assistant wrapped up the glass bear for me.

Some kiss. I tried not to think of Tim too much.

Instead I counted out the notes carefully and handed them over. I'd never had so much money in my hand before but it didn't seem to mean anything. All the transaction meant was there was a gap on the shop's shelf now, and something heavy in my hand. That was it.

I'd dreamt of having this glass bear so often, but now it was mine it wasn't the same any more. It wasn't even icy. I had a feel of it before the assistant had wrapped it up and the glass was warm from the spot lights.

I swung the bag from my arm as I walked to the park with Mata straining on the leash I held tight in the other hand.

I had to find Tim again. Not the Tim they'd left in his place, but my Tim. My special adviser. The one who crept out to give me Mata. He was the only person who would understand what I had to do. And the only way I could get hold of him was to wait at the Seize the Day bench.

I was going to leave the white glass bear sitting in the grass under the bench. It would be my message for Tim. I wanted him to know I needed him now. I wanted to be free. If he ever needed a mission, then I was it.

I breathed, my hands splayed out on my diaphragm. In, and I could feel my ribs expand under my fingers; out, and I was in danger of touching my backbone.

Iced inside. Ice melting. An unspoilt world. Anything had to be possible.

I was walking back to the shop trying to work out what to do next when I saw Joe.

I shouted his name and he turned. He really did. He saw me, and then he ducked into the alley. This time there was no mistaking the fact he was avoiding me. I stood against the wall, kicking the bricks again and again with the backs of my boots, my fists hitting the rough edges until I felt the skin on my hands tear. I wanted to bruise myself against all the words I could no longer hear.

Watch out, Tim had told me. It'll always be the ones you don't expect. I suddenly knew it was Joe who had told my father where I was. But had he done it on his own? What if Miranda had been in on it too? What if Tim was right, and there really was no one I could trust? Had she balanced things up, and offered Joe my future for the chance of him helping her find a new one for her?

I waited to see if Joe would appear again and then, when he didn't, started to walk slowly, keeping to the edges of the pavement until I got to Miranda's front gate. I was pulling Mata along, muttering to her the whole way. I had to keep myself in control.

FORTY-FIVE

Miranda's dad was watching the wrestling. All four bars of the gas fire were on and Mata was lying asleep on the rug in front, as close to the heat as she could get.

With everything that was happening, it wasn't surprising I was finding it hard to concentrate. I'd already gone through to ask Mrs Bartlett – 'call me Fran' – if she wanted a hand, but she'd whooshed me away and told me to keep Mr Bartlett – 'him you can call stupid. No, only joking, Neil will do. It's his name, after all' – company while I waited for Miranda to come home. Fran said it would be like old times for Mr Bartlett. Miranda always used to enjoy watching the wrestling with her father in the afternoons. It was one of the many things they used to do as a family. Before things changed, Fran said, giving me a sharp look.

'What's happening?' I asked Mr Bartlett, Neil. I was trying to be one of the family. Miranda wouldn't see me out on the streets. She'd said that.

'They're such characters,' he laughed. On the screen, one masked fat man was knocking the head of a pony-tailed fat man against the ground, while yet another fat man in a striped shirt was pointing a finger over them.

I tried to look amused but Neil must have seen through this because he ignored me and offered no more explanations. A series of controls on the arm of his wheelchair allowed him to move backwards and forwards, and he did this constantly, shifting first an inch to one side, and then two inches to the other. I could see holes everywhere in the carpet which suggested this was a habit.

'I want the masked man to win,' I said, half-wondering why it had taken Miranda so long to stop enjoying the wrestling.

'Why?' I'd obviously picked the wrong one. Neil looked not so much surprised as irritated.

'No reason really. Although it's quite mysterious, isn't it? He's probably hiding some horrible injury which would mean he wouldn't be on television if he couldn't wear a mask. It's probably a bit of a dream come true for him.'

'An ugly mug more like. It's just a gimmick, a ploy to make you notice him. The other guy's got more talent in his little finger.' Neil turned his attention back to his wheelchair controls. 'Fran,' he shouted. 'What do you have to do round here to get a cup of tea? I'm parched.'

'Can't you get it yourself?' I asked.

I was genuinely interested, but Neil just glared at me and didn't answer. 'Fran,' he called again.

I went through to the kitchen. Fran was sitting at the table, sucking the top of her pen as she studied a crossword puzzle in one of the magazines Miranda always used to read. 'Mr Bartlett wants a cup of tea,' I said sweetly. 'Shall I make him one?'

'Better not,' she said. 'Too many liquids after lunch and he'll be up all night.'

I held on to the back of one of the chairs, hoping she'd ask me to sit down but she didn't. When was Miranda coming back?

'My mum used to do crossword puzzles,' I said eventually. 'Sometimes she'd let me help her.'

Fran nodded but still didn't look up. I could smell the vanilla sweetness of cake baking in the oven, touched with ginger and cinnamon. A bright red and white checked mug was sitting in front of Fran, and she was stirring it constantly so the spoon banged against the china rhythmically. From the other room, I could hear Neil shouting out for more blood and more tea, seemingly making no distinction between the kitchen and the television screen.

Fran snorted.

'Men,' I said sympathetically, shaking my head.

'So how's your boyfriend?' Fran asked.

'Fine,' I tried to sound positive. 'Has Miranda got a boyfriend?' Please don't let him be called Joe, I wanted to say. Please don't let Miranda have lied to me and given away all my secrets.

Fran's spoon almost shattered the mug. 'She hasn't had one since that bloody teacher,' she said. 'She's told you about him, I suppose.'

I nodded. I was just about to say how romantic it all sounded but just then Neil screamed next door for the wrestler to really bloody that mask and I shut up.

'What's Miranda's secret, Fran?'

'Secret?'

'The last time I was here you said she was being secretive, getting letters and stuff? It's just that I thought you and she told each other everything.'

Fran laughed. 'That,' she said. 'It was only about college. She wanted to wait until it was all settled before telling me. Didn't want me to think that all that teacher stuff was happening again and start worrying all over again. A friend of yours helped her as it happened.'

'A boy?'

'Joe. That was his name. To be honest, and I hope you don't mind me saying, Miranda didn't really care for him. They fell out, anyway. Miranda doesn't like nosey people. She's been a great one for minding her own business since Mr Don't-Let-Me-Ever-Catch-Him Sullivan and his la-di-da ideas. Going to take her to France, he was. Have you ever heard the like? The headmaster hadn't when I went to see him to give him the lowdown, that's for sure. I threatened the police.'

'So Joe was asking questions? About me? And Miranda didn't tell him anything?'

'Talk about pot calling the kettle black.' Fran stood up. 'I'm starting to feel I'm in the middle of a bloody inquisition here.'

'When's Miranda coming back?' I cursed myself. Another question.

'Why don't you wait for her upstairs in her room.' Fran raised her eyebrows. 'At least you won't have to hear Mr Let's-Have-More-Blood up there.'

I bounced up and down on Miranda's bed first of all, relishing the distance it was from the floor. I'd been sleeping on a mattress for so long I'd forgotten what it felt like.

Then I went over to the dressing table and picked up a white jewellery box. I opened it slowly, but the ballerina still popped up and started pirouetting hopefully, her arms straight above her head. Miranda's jewellery was the sort a child gets given on special occasions. A gold crucifix, a tiny ring with the smallest pearl I'd ever seen, a silver bracelet that expanded to slip over the hand.

I put them all carefully back and folded the ballerina down before I shut the box. The three dolls were still up there on top of Miranda's wardrobe. They watched me with glassy unblinking eyes. Her clothes were hanging on wooden hangers, all facing the same way and colour co-ordinated from black to blue to beige to white. One red dress stood out, and I held it against me in front of the mirror. Miranda's shoes were lined up at the bottom of the wardrobe, each paired up and held firm with a wooden shoe-tree.

I looked through Miranda's books. The titles on the top three shelves covered every emotion from love to hate. Women yearned in the arms of big men on front covers. The only break from the uniform pastel shades and neat line of books was at the end of the row, where five hard-backed children's books stood out clumsily, dog-eared, torn and obviously much read. Miranda had told me once that she was keeping things for her kids. I guessed these were part of the inheritance. On impulse I picked one out, and put it in my rucksack.

The books on the bottom two shelves must have been from Miranda's course. They were bulging with Post-it notes and scraps of hand-written paper. I picked out an old battered paperback that seemed to be standing on its own, *Tess of the D'Urbervilles*, and turned to the inside page.

Thomas Sullivan, English Dept.

So I wasn't the only one who stole books.

I could hear the phone ringing downstairs as I lay on the floor and looked under the bed.

There were bags and bags squeezed under there. All made of black cardboard, and all tied with the same black ribbon as the one she'd given me before. I pulled one out and tore off the packaging. I couldn't help but gasp as I opened it up. A jewelled jacket of pink and black and gold tweed nestled in black tissue paper. I took it out gently and ran my finger down the row of black silk buttons, each one embossed with the designer's logo. Even the lining was beautiful. I rubbed the thick pink silk against my cheek.

In the next bag, there was an emerald green satin evening dress. Halter-necked, full-skirted. A red cashmere cardigan was folded in the third; a pair of grey woollen trousers in the fourth; I draped the black crepe dress I pulled out of the fifth bag against my shoulders, fingered the buttons, airbrushed the waist. All of these clothes unworn, still with their labels on. I'd be willing to bet Miranda hadn't even tried them on.

They were clothes not just for an older woman than Miranda,

but for a woman with a different life. A woman who would go to places like St Tropez, and stay out until morning. I remembered Miranda's face as she watched me try on that dress the first time I came here. That look of love I'd recognised. Miranda didn't want my stories because she'd wanted to keep hers intact. She'd never given up hope of Mr Thomas Sullivan knocking on her door.

I swept all of the clothes into one of the bags and cleaned the rest of the tissue paper and empty bags away back under the bed so she wouldn't notice immediately. She'd be better off without all those wishful thoughts creeping up through her mattress and into her dreams every time she slept. If he was going to turn up, he would. But in the meantime, Miranda had a chance for something better.

'That was Miranda.' Fran popped out of the kitchen as I came downstairs, drying her hands on a tea towel. 'She's going to be late back. Out with her friends. Other friends,' she corrected herself.

'That's OK.' I was trying to manoeuvre past her and out of the door so she wouldn't see the bag I was carrying.

'Do you want to leave a message?'

'No, it's OK.' I was nearly at the door. I had to get out otherwise I'd want to stay there with Fran looking after me for ever and now I knew Miranda hadn't stolen my future, I owed it to her to leave. She was no Leanne. I couldn't look to her to protect me. At least one of us could have the chance of real life. And wasn't I an expert at this? Moving on.

'Haven't you forgotten something?' Fran was laughing. 'What about your dog?'

Mata growled as I picked her up and tucked her under my arm. She didn't want to go. On the television, the wrestling had finished. Now a curiously orange man was screaming with excitement as a bespectacled woman fitted different coloured shapes into holes. The studio audience were clapping and Neil's chair was rocking in rhythm.

'Turn it off,' he pleaded. 'Please.'

I ignored him. There was no need for him to ignore me as if I didn't exist.

'We're off now,' I shouted out to Fran as I left. 'Mata and I.'

FORTY-SIX

Dawn was on reception again when I walked into Summerfields.

'Hello,' she grinned. Her hair was even messier than last time. Did she try to style it like that? 'A little visitor. How lovely.'

If I found Dawn annoying, what must the residents think of her? Still at least she remembered me.

'So how can we help you? You haven't been here before, have you?' she asked then. 'Who are you here to see?'

'I know the way to the room,' I said.

'I'm not sure—'

But it was too late. I was already on my way down the corridor.

There was no answer when I knocked on Mr Roberts's door, so I pushed it open gently. How many people must have stood like this before going into one of these rooms, bracing themselves for what they'd find inside? 'He's not himself today,' they'd say, trying to pretend that the self they were seeing was only a pretend one and that the young, more vital person they wanted to remember would miraculously appear the next time they visited. That he'd be 'himself' again.

Mr Roberts was asleep. His white hands were crossed over the fold of the top sheet as if in prayer. His breath was coming out in sharp, painful sounding jolts. I pulled the chair over to his side, knocking over a bin as I did so.

He opened one eye. 'Molly,' he said, before closing it again. A photograph of him and Mrs Roberts stood on the bedside table.

It must have been taken a long time ago at one of those old-fashioned seaside amusement parks. Mr Roberts was poking his head through a hole in a painted board so he looked as if he was an astronaut perched on a rocket, while Mrs Roberts stood to one side, a headscarf tied tightly round her head, handbag clamped to her side. It was noticeable that while he was grinning towards the camera, Mrs Roberts was caught looking down at her feet. I could tell she disapproved of his high jinks.

Somehow this gave me courage. 'Nice photo,' I said. 'One small step and all that.'

He coughed and reached for his handkerchief, knocking the glass of water slightly so it trembled but didn't spill.

'Too tired.' Mr Roberts spoke haltingly, as if each word was emerging raw and sharp from his throat. 'Is it time?'

'I wanted to tell you a story,' I said.

First of all, he shook his head an inch to each side, and then shut his eyes again. 'Special story. Had enough.'

'Enough stories?' I asked, but he shook his head again.

'Leanne.'

'That's right. Little Leanne.' I sat back in the chair and steepled my fingers under my chin. My skin felt soft and squashy against my nails. 'She needs help. You understand that, don't you?'

'Please.' He shut his eyes as I began talking. It was the story of how things never went right for Leanne. Everything she tried to do was taken the wrong way. People always expected the worst from her so what happened was that's what she ended up giving to them. She hid all the bad things she did well though, because at the back of her mind she always kept the hope that everyone else could be wrong, and maybe she would be all right in the end. Plus she had one friend who helped her.

'You,' Mr Roberts half-smiled.

'Me,' I nodded. 'One day though she decided to leave her family and set off on her own. She was scared and lonely but then she met up with an older man who offered to help her.'

'Kind?' Mr Roberts's eyelids were translucent, but when I waved my hand over his face he didn't flinch. I allowed him his interruptions this time. They would stop him falling asleep, and would only improve the effect of this particular story.

'The man was kind to Leanne but only up to a point,' I continued. 'He kept her in a room above his business, and would visit her there from time to time.'

Mr Roberts said something I couldn't hear. I leant over him as he repeated it. 'Bastard.'

'Maybe,' I said. 'Maybe not.' I was watching the flush rise up his neck. His hand fluttered round his chest, before settling on his heart. It looked like a claw there, the fingers turning in on each other.

'But the strange thing was that Leanne grew fond of this older man. He was never unkind or cruel or anything to her, and after he'd done his stuff with her' – Mr Roberts snorted – 'he'd stay with her, letting her curl herself into a little ball on his lap and stroking her shoulder gently. He would play with her hair, outline the shape of her body with his fingers, leave little kisses across her neck. He'd hold her close.'

Mr Roberts sighed, and I paused for a moment to let him think about this. 'He'd bring treats every day for Leanne,' I went on. 'Soaps smelling of lavender and sandalwood for her to bathe with, heart-shaped chocolates that tasted of real mint, handmade paper too good to write on with rose petals pressed into it, the smallest embroidered velvet shoes you've ever seen.'

'Little feet,' Mr Roberts nodded. 'S'right.' I thought back. I couldn't remember ever mentioning the size of Leanne's feet before. Mr Roberts was smiling now, his eyes shut tight.

'Do you want me to go on? I won't if you don't want,' I asked but he nodded. It was time to up the tempo.

'One day though, the man came to see Leanne and said he didn't have any money any more. That she couldn't stay living in her little room but would have to go out into the streets with everyone else. She wasn't going to be special any more.'

'Leanne was crying but there was nowhere else for her to go. She bumped into the man's friend. A big ugly man whom Leanne hated. An angry man and there was nothing the first man could do about it. Leanne had to eat and he had no money to give her. He didn't even have a potato.'

Mr Roberts opened his eyes. I ignored him and concentrated instead on a spot on the carpet.

'The ugly man laughed as he saw Leanne cowering on the bed. He told her to take off all her clothes and watched as she stood there cold and naked. He even forced her to put her hands on her head and turn round slowly in front of him, while he appraised her as critically as he might an object he'd just bought. He even clucked as if he wasn't completely happy with his purchase.

'Leanne was crying all this time,' I said. 'Tears were pouring down her cheeks, but she wasn't allowed to mop them up.'

Mr Roberts let out a grunt. I still didn't let myself look at him, but I was sure he was crying too. I carried on looking at the spot on the carpet. What I wanted to capture was the same helpless horror I'd felt when I read the description of the Amsterdam prostitute, the same hopelessness I reacted to in *The Story of O*.

I forced myself to carry on with the story.

'He made Leanne walk to his car like that. He strapped her in the back seat, and blindfolded her, tying her wrists with a light silk scarf. He took her to a house and led her straight to the basement. Leanne could hear the sound of angry voices – male voices – somewhere from upstairs. She was scared. Poor, poor little Leanne. Someone came and dragged her roughly over to the bed before locking the door with a series of clinking keys. There was no one to rescue her. It was too late for that now. She was nothing.'

Suddenly there was a cry from the bed. Mr Roberts was clutching at his heart. His breath was both quick and laboured. He whistled every time he breathed in, gasped as he breathed out.

I got up and walked over to the basin, and filled up the glass with water. After I'd drunk it, I went back to the bed.

'But she got out,' I whispered. 'Look, she's here now. I rescued her. It's all right.' I pulled the sheet up and gently covered Mr Roberts up to his chin. 'And Mrs Roberts will be all right now. You don't need to worry about her any more. I'll look after her.' My fingers trailed over his clammy forehead. He was staring up at me. I put one finger on his mouth as if to hush him.

'Women like her always survive,' I said. 'Sometimes they meet men like you. Sometimes they're not so lucky. It's for the best.' I was telling myself this as much as him. 'Everything is for the best.'

He nodded, and then he shut his eyes.

Dawn looked up as I passed the reception. 'He wants to be left alone for the rest of the afternoon,' I said. 'Mrs Roberts is coming in later and I made sure he's got everything he needs.'

Dawn smiled. 'Well, I'm sure he enjoyed such a lovely visit,' she said.

Mata was still guarding the bag outside. She whimpered as I came near, but I didn't untie her. Instead I took the bag back inside.

'I was wondering if you'd like these,' I said. 'They don't fit me any more and I was just going to take them to the charity shop.'

Pity there wouldn't be a next time because I was sure she'd remember me now. It felt good too not to be carrying the burden of Miranda's dream any more, and when I looked back I could see Dawn holding the green satin dress up to her body, twirling round in front of the window and smiling at her reflection.

FORTY-SEVEN

By the time Mata and I reached the Seize the Day bench, it was dark. I tried different opening sentences out on Mata, making my face look bright and animated. We sat down on a bench and I practised laughing, the way I had seen other women do, holding up my chin so my neck appeared elongated. I forced myself not to look down and see if the bear was still there.

'And where are you going this summer?' I said loudly in my best tea party voice.

All the time I was looking for men, or of course one man in particular. Not that I was any more. Particular. I hitched the skirt of my dress up so I was showing even the bit at the top of my leg where the bruises were healing, but still no one approached. I stroked my skin in a circular motion. Although it didn't give me the same jolt as the pinching, it was still satisfying.

'Do you come here often?' I asked Mata, who was sitting beside me on the bench, guarding against spooks in the half-light.

I was just about to give up when a shadow blocked mine from behind. Mata growled but only a light growl. Tim, I thought, my stomach lifting up with excitement. I'd tell him he'd got better at surprising me, that I really hadn't seen him come this time. I forced myself not to turn, but continued to rub my legs, round and round. Mata continued to growl softly but I hushed her down. 'It's all right,' I said, not sure exactly who I was trying to comfort. I could smell a sweet scent, over-ripe plums mixed with Parma violets.

247

I closed my eyes, better to take this in but when I opened them again, I could see only blackness. The branches of Jessica's tree stretched out above me. The stars were visible through them, the silver coin of the moon, and in between a canopy of coloured shapes and ribbons, arching over me, protecting me.

Liz would be pottering round her lonely home, a book propped up in front of her ready meal for one and surprising herself by feeling grateful for having at least another go at life. Miranda would be at the pub with her new friends talking about the future. Mrs Roberts would be mourning Mr Roberts, genuinely, lovingly but with a spark of relief that maybe now at least she'd find some freedom.

If I could make all that happen then maybe other things could turn out differently too.

There was one iced white heart I'd never noticed before on the tree. It was twisting this way and that on its golden thread as it gave itself up to the gust of freezing wind that blew suddenly through the park, and which I felt in my bones.

'You?' I asked when I felt the hand on my shoulder. Even before she replied, I knew exactly who I wanted it to be. When she came to sit next to me on the bench, I let my body mould into hers so there was no air between us.

'Sweetheart,' she whispered, as she stroked my hair. And then she looked straight at me as if I wasn't bad any more, but actually someone rather good. After that, there was no need for either of us to say anything else at all.

ACKNOWLEDGEMENTS

Grateful thanks are due to the many people who kept me going in different ways, both large and small, while I wrote this book including Mary Atkinson, Christopher Barker, Nicholas Bate, Gillie Bolton, Café Divine, the Clink Street group, Alice Elliot Dark, Sue Davis, James Friel, Alison Grant, Corinna Harrod, Deborah Heath, Rupert Heath, Celia Hunt, Alex Johnson, Anne Kelly, Dorothy Ledsham, Shaun Levin, Michelle Lovric, Mo McAuley, Cheryl Moskowitz, Scott Pack, Henry Peplow, Reginald Peplow, Stephen Peplow, Lynne Rees, Ann Salway, Francis Salway, Hugh Salway, Rachael Salway, Catherine Smith, Christine Terris, Susan Wicks, and everyone at the Virginia Center for Creative Arts.